## 'You're a ——, Julie!'

'I beg your ——————— on talking about ——————— of being provocative ——————

'Are you ever true to one person, Julie?'

'I think you're crazy,' she said sharply. 'I think you're trying to cover up your own weakness.'

Blue eyes narrowed warningly. 'Weakness, Julie?'

'Yes, weakness,' she snapped. 'Only a man with no self-control would kiss a—a woman who isn't free!'

Born in the industrial heart of England, **Margaret Mayo** now lives with her husband in a pretty Staffordshire canalside village. Once a secretary, she turned her hand to writing her books both at home and in exotic locations, combining her hobby of photography with her research.

**Recent titles by the same author:**

DETERMINED LADY

# STOLEN
# FEELINGS

BY

MARGARET MAYO

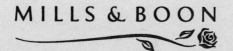

MILLS & BOON

*All the characters in this book have no existence outside the
imagination of the author, and have no relation whatsoever to anyone
bearing the same name or names. They are not even distantly inspired
by any individual known or unknown to the author, and all the
incidents are pure invention.*

MILLS & BOON and the Rose Device
are trademarks of the publisher.
Harlequin Mills & Boon Limited,
Eton House, 18–24 Paradise Road, Richmond, Surrey TW9 1SR

© Margaret Mayo 1995

ISBN 0 263 79349 4

Set in 10 on 12 pt Linotron Times
01-9601-53757

Typeset in Great Britain by CentraCet, Cambridge
Made and printed in Great Britain

# CHAPTER ONE

JULIE found her patience growing thin. Where the devil was Ian? He had promised to meet her. She had stood here for almost half an hour in the searing heat and, apart from a handful of people going about their daily business, the small harbour was deserted.

She heard the Jeep before it came into sight. It sounded as though it was being driven flat out, as though someone was in a great hurry. She watched frowningly as the vehicle came hurtling towards her, as the brakes were slammed on and the Jeep swung around so that it was ready to take off again.

The man who jumped out was much taller and broader than her brother, packed with hard muscle, deeply tanned, with jet-black hair cut brutally short. He looked at her piercingly and questioningly for several seconds, as if he was not entirely sure that she was the person he had come to pick up. 'Julie Drummond?' There was something in his tone that sounded odd, and his harsh, frowning face suggested that he was not happy about having to make this journey.

Julie was tall also, but she nevertheless needed to lift her head to look up at this man. 'Yes, that's me,' she declared firmly.

His eyes narrowed on her unnervingly for a second before he growled, 'Let's get going.' He picked up her suitcase and tossed it unceremoniously into the back of the battered Jeep, waited with obvious impatience while she clambered in, and then took off again at the same breakneck speed.

'I do want to get there in one piece,' Julie announced testily, bracing herself with both hands. She was already bad-tempered at being kept waiting and this man was putting the fear of hell into her.

A pair of the deepest blue eyes she had ever seen swivelled in her direction. They were the nicest part about him, she decided; the rest of his face was all hard, uncompromising angles. 'You're quite safe,' he told her coldly.

It didn't feel like it to her. 'What's the hurry?' she questioned.

'I have other more important things to do,' came the harsh response.

'And you object to being sent to pick me up, is that it?' she asked sharply. 'Where's Ian? I thought he was coming?' This man was totally objectionable. She was dusty and hot and tired, her long black hair clung limply and damply to her head, instead of cascading in its usual riot of waves, and the last thing she wanted was to feel unwelcome.

'Your *husband* is stranded on Pinzón,' he told her. 'He should have returned last night but the boat developed engine trouble. He will hopefully be back later today.'

Julie did not like the emphasis he put on the word 'husband'—almost as though he knew that she was masquerading as Ian's wife! There was no way he could, of course, unless Ian himself had said something, and that was unlikely; it had to be her conscience. But she touched the wedding-ring she was wearing, twisting it uneasily. It was a cheap one, bought to add credibility to their story, and it did not feel right on her finger.

When her twin brother had first applied for the job as Cameron Storm's research assistant in the Galapagos Islands he hadn't realised that the eminent ecologist was seeking a husband and wife team.

'He apparently needs someone to type out his notes and maintain accurate daily records,' Ian had told her when he returned from his interview, 'and also to do the cooking.'

'A cook?' Julie had looked at her brother in astonishment. 'You're asking me to come with you as Cameron Storm's *cook*? Heavens, Ian, that's not my line at all.'

'But you are looking for a job; you know you hate being out of work, and you are an accomplished typist,' he'd pointed out. 'This means such a lot to me.'

Her brother, also interested in ecology, but nowhere near as experienced and knowledgeable as Cameron Storm, was besotted with the idea of going out to the Galapagos Islands. He had been ever since, as a schoolboy, he'd read about Charles Darwin's visit there.

Although Ian and Julie were roughly the same height, his hair was not quite so dark, and he had a rounder face and a much stockier figure; they didn't even look like brother and sister, let alone twins.

'There's so much to find out,' he said to Julie. 'A short holiday would serve no purpose. I need to be able to live there to do any good.'

They shared the same house in the village of Barlaston in Staffordshire, England, where the great Wedgwood pottery factory was situated. The Wedgwoods and the Darwins had always been great friends and there had been a lot of intermarriage between the two families over the years—Charles

Darwin marrying his cousin, Emma Wedgwood, in the 1830s.

It was this vague connection with Charles Darwin and Barlaston that had increased her brother's interest, even though Charles Darwin had lived in Shrewsbury as a young man. 'I'll never get another chance to work with someone as expert and experienced as Cameron Storm,' he went on. 'I shall learn so much—it's fantastic. Please, please say you'll come.'

'It could be what I need, I suppose,' said Julie. In fact, it was the perfect escape, but she wasn't telling Ian that yet. Immersing herself in a new job and new surroundings would be a great help in trying to forget her bitter break-up with Roger. It was the deceit that troubled her—pretending to be married; she did not like that one little bit.

'Didn't you tell Cameron Storm that you and Julie had split up?' she asked Ian. It was confusing that her sister-in-law had the same Christian name, though convenient for Ian, now that he wanted her to masquerade as his wife.

'Goodness, no!' he exclaimed. 'The man believes in the sanctity of marriage. He thinks it should be for life.'

'Is he not married himself?'

Ian shook his head.

'Why? Is he as ugly as sin? Will no one have him?'

'Hardly,' laughed Ian. 'He's a handsome devil but he's dedicated to his work. I don't think he wants the complications of a single girl on the team. Too many of them make a bee-line for him.'

'So why doesn't he get a male secretary?' Julie asked. 'And a male cook?'

'I don't know,' replied Ian tetchily. 'All I know is

that he said the job's mine if Julie comes with me. But Julie can't come, can she? So I want you to take her place.' He gave one of his most appealing smiles. 'We're so close, Sis, no one will ever know.'

He was right, they were close; they always had been. More so when their parents had divorced fifteen years ago, when she and Ian were only eleven years old. Oddly, there had never been any indication that there was anything wrong with their parents' marriage—no arguments, no bad vibes, nothing—until the day their father had upped and gone, and that was the last she and Ian had seen of him.

The break-up had remained a mystery, their mother always maintaining a strict silence about the whole affair, but Julie guessed that her father had gone off with another woman. It was only now that Ian had experienced a similar trauma, and she was trying to deal with her own broken affair, that Julie was learning to understand how much her mother had suffered.

'What if Cameron Storm finds out I'm not your wife?' she asked her brother worriedly.

'How will he?' he fenced. 'You've both the same name, so there's no chance of a slip-up there, and although I have met Cameron in the past he's never met Julie. There's no possible way he can find out. Oh, please, Sis, my life depends on it.'

He was being overly dramatic, but Julie had been concerned about her twin ever since his wife had walked out. She had actually never felt the other Julie was right for him, but he had been besotted, and before they had known each other three months they were married.

He had never stopped loving her either, she truly was the only girl in the world for him, but her eye had strayed after less than eighteen months of marriage, and Ian had arrived home from work one day to discover that she had run off with his best friend.

He had been distraught and had come to his sister in tears. He had even been prepared to forgive his wife but she had announced that their marriage was over, that she did not love him any more and that she wanted a divorce.

Today was the first time Julie had seen her brother show enthusiasm for anything since—but, even though she felt quite excited herself at the thought of going out to the Galapagos Islands, she was still not convinced that pretending to be her brother's wife was a good thing to do. Surely honesty would be the best policy?

'Just think of it as one big, long holiday,' he urged. 'You'll be able to completely forget that swine Roger. You'll be able to relax totally while we're out in the field, and I doubt Cameron's notes will be vast. You'll be able to sunbathe and swim and generally enjoy yourself.'

Finally she had dispelled her misgivings and agreed, and now here she was, sitting beside this big, irritating man, almost melting with the heat, resenting the fact that he looked as cool and comfortable as it if were springtime in England.

'And who are you?' she asked, hoping the whole team wasn't going to be as hostile. She had envisaged a happy, friendly group of people, had let Ian persuade her that the whole thing would be fun. She could only hope that no one else would be this disagreeable.

She had looked the Galapagos Islands up when her brother had first mentioned them—in the Pacific, all volcanic, belonging to Ecuador, straddling the equator, almost totally a National Park, only of significance to people who were interested in natural history.

Thick brows rose. 'I'm sorry, didn't I introduce myself?' A faint mocking smile curved a mouth that was generously wide. 'I'm Cameron Storm.'

'Oh!' Julie swallowed hard. 'I didn't realise.'

'Obviously.'

She tried to think what she had said to him, and hoped she hadn't jeopardised her brother's chances.

'Ian didn't tell me what a firebrand you were. I have a good team here, *Mrs* Drummond. I hope you're not going to disrupt things with your hasty temper?'

There it was again, a veiled reference to her marital status. Julie began to feel worried, but she showed none of it; she had to speak to Ian first. 'I don't have a hasty temper,' she fired back, and then laughed. 'Standing around for half an hour in this heat isn't my idea of fun. I'd begun to think Ian had forgotten I was arriving today.'

'Ian didn't forget,' he reassured her. 'He was desperately worried when he couldn't get back—you're a very lucky woman having a man love you so much.' His eyes were watchful on her face as he spoke. 'We have a radio system, of course, to keep in touch with each other, and he asked if someone else could pick you up.'

'You didn't have to come yourself,' she pointed out.

'I was the only man at camp.'

'I'm sorry if I've inconvenienced you.' She rested her hazel eyes on him for a brief moment. So this was Cameron Storm, the man her brother deeply admired and respected. Ian had said he was handsome and she couldn't deny that, but he had failed to tell her that he was an impatient man also, that he didn't like things that upset his routine, and he certainly wasn't happy about having to fetch her today.

'Forget it, Mrs Drummond, it's done now.'

'Please, call me Julie.' The deception, which had always bothered her, was disturbing her more with each second that passed.

'Here we are.' He brought the Jeep to a shuddering halt at a campsite set well back on a white sandy beach, brown canvas tents pitched in regimental order.

Julie looked at the scene in complete and utter dismay. 'Is this it? Is this where we're to live?' She was unable to hide her consternation, feeling suddenly let down. Ian could have told her. He had let her come out here without giving her any idea at all that she would be expected to rough it for the next twelve months.

Dark, mocking brows rose. 'What did you expect, the Ritz?' And he looked her up and down in her obviously expensive white dress and the totally impractical high-heeled sandals.

Her eyes flashed. 'No one told me.'

'Then blame Ian, not me,' he retorted. 'Let me show you your tent.'

Most of them were open-sided, but the one he took her to in the far corner was thankfully enclosed and would afford her some degree of privacy—until she poked her head inside and saw Ian's possessions! She almost blurted out there and then that she and Ian weren't married, only the fact that she knew her twin would be furious stopping her. She had already done enough damage by speaking to Cameron Storm as though he was a nobody.

'I'll leave you to get settled,' he said, a touch of humour lurking on his lips.

Julie looked into the intent blueness of his eyes, and to her utter, utter astonishment felt a faint pull of atttraction. Lord, what was happening? Something like this would be fatal; it would completely ruin her brother's chances of staying here and furthering his career.

Besides, she had come out here to get over Roger, not to trip headlong into another relationship. Her chin came up. 'And then what?' She did not realise how aggressive her voice sounded.

An eyebrow slid smoothly upwards. 'Nothing much for today. I'll show you the tent I use as an office and when Raul, our present cook, returns you will be able to see how things are run in the kitchen.'

Julie frowned, a suspicion dawning. 'How many am I expected to cook for?'

'Why, all of us.' He looked surprised at her question.

'And how many is all of us?'

'At the moment about twenty.'

'Twenty?' she echoed. 'I didn't know that; it wasn't the impression I got. I actually thought, naïve as it seems, that you'd rented a house and needed a cook-cum-typist.'

He gave a bark of laughter, and it was surprising how it softened the harsh lines of his face and made him look more human. 'Actually you're half right. You, Ian and myself are moving to Isla Fragata, or Vulcan Island as it is more commonly known.'

'Just the three of us?' she asked cautiously.

'Yes.' He grew serious again. 'It should prove very—interesting, from many points of view. Ian is very eager to learn, but——' his tone sharpened '—his success depends upon you.'

Julie frowned. 'Me? What do you mean?'

'You're fully aware of my stipulation?'

'That you wouldn't take him on your team if I didn't come too?'

'That's right.'

'I can't understand why,' Julie said strongly. 'If you're afraid of being chased by single girls you could have employed a man.'

'Afraid, Mrs Drummond? Me?' He looked considerably amused.

Julie shrugged. 'Ian said that was the reason.'

Cameron Storm's mouth twisted cynically. 'I suppose it was a natural assumption, but he's wide of the mark. The truth is I did not think it fair to part him from his wife for twelve long months; it could put his—marriage in jeopardy.'

He paused a moment, as though expecting her to say something. Julie hid her unease but remained silent. He couldn't possibly know that she wasn't Ian's wife, she was being too sensitive.

'Besides,' he went on briskly, 'I happened to need someone with your qualifications. You can—er—type, I presume?'

Julie inclined her head, her eyes flashing her impatience at such a question.

'You're not exactly what I expected,' he added surprisingly. 'I rather thought Ian's wife was a blonde; I don't know why. But then——' he grinned widely, showing amazingly white teeth '—it's amazing what you can get out of a bottle.'

Julie could not believe this man. He was totally confusing her and she wanted to get away from him, she wanted to speak to Ian, she wanted to ask him what, if anything, he had said. God, already it was so difficult.

'All I ask,' he said, the humour gone now, his voice brusque, 'is that you don't let your husband down.'

Taken by surprise, she asked sharply, 'And what is that supposed to mean?'

'I think you know.' His blue eyes narrowed upon hers and Julie felt a quiver of unease. Another thought struck her. Surely he wasn't aware that she already felt a faint pull of attraction? Surely she hadn't given herself away in this short space of time? He didn't think, he *couldn't* think, that she was like this with every man she met? Could he?

'If you can't cope,' he added crisply, 'say so now and you and Ian can go back to England before we get started.'

Julie deliberately misinterpreted him. 'I have no doubt at all that I can cope with the job.' It had taken them ages to get their permits to stay and work here; Ian would never forgive her if she fouled things up now.

'And everything else?' he persisted, and this time there was no doubt what he meant.

'But of course.' She kept her eyes steady on his.

'And may I suggest that you do something with your hair.' His eyes raked over its long length. 'Either tie it up or get the scissors to it. It's totally impractical in this heat.'

She tossed her head. 'You don't have to tell me, I've already found that out. I have every intention of tying my hair back just as soon as I've had a shower and changed.'

'Showered?' He looked at her as though she were out of her mind. 'There are no mod cons here.'

Julie felt slightly foolish, but she was damned if she

would show it. She lifted her chin defensively.
'Whatever.'

In the privacy of the tent Julie flung herself down on
one of the camp-beds and wondered what she had let
herself in for. Apart from the difficulty of the masquerade, she had never imagined anything like this. Had
Ian known they would be sleeping under canvas? Had
he deliberately misled her? Or had he thought it would
be different too?

Throughout the flight from England to Ecuador she
had tried to imagine what life in the Galapagos Islands
would be like. Nothing had prepared her for camping
out on the beach. She actually did not like sleeping
under canvas.

When they were young, she and Ian had gone on
a camping holiday with their parents and a violent
thunderstorm had blown down the tent in the middle
of the night. Several dozen frightened cows had come
charging through their camp and frightened her even
more than the storm. They had never managed to
persuade her to sleep under canvas again.

It was a pity, Julie thought now, that she and Ian
had not been able to fly out here together. They'd
actually had difficulty in getting flights, and in the end
he had come out more than a week before her.

She had stayed one night in Ecuador at a hotel in
Quito, and had somehow expected things to be equally
as civilised here. Perhaps, if she had thought about it
properly, she would have realised that it wasn't possible, that living in a tent was far more practical when
it was necessary to move camp from one island to
another—except that she hadn't known they would be
moving!

It was hot inside the tent and totally airless, and it

was easy to see why most of them had no sides—obviously Cameron had thought that she and Ian needed their privacy!

Eventually she sat up and hugged her knees and looked about her. There was not exactly a lot of room and only one small area to store and hang their clothes. She had brought far too much, most of it totally impractical. When would she ever wear dresses, for instance? And high heels? She had thought they would dine out sometimes, that it wouldn't be all work and no play. It certainly didn't look like that now.

She knew that Santa Cruz was the second largest island and the main tourist centre, with the Charles Darwin Research Station stituated here, but she hadn't really understood how remote their camp was going to be. And she was afraid to imagine what it was going to be like when they went to Vulcan Island. The stress would be intolerable.

Julie pulled off her dress and contemplated slipping into the sea as she desperately needed to cool down. Then the thought that Cameron Storm might be out there watching made her quickly change her mind. She would manage without, for the time being.

She opened her suitcase and tugged out a T-shirt and shorts. She saw no point at all in unpacking if they would shortly be on the move. She fished her comb out of her bag and raked it through her hair, twisting its length into a knot on top of her head which she fixed securely with a few hairpins.

When she ventured outside, Cameron, surprisingly and pleasingly, was nowhere in sight and she was able to wander through the campsite at will. She found the kitchen supplies tent and a stove that was run by Calor gas, which she supposed she was going to have to learn to use.

Intense fury ran through her. She wasn't the world's best cook, and it wasn't a task she particularly enjoyed. If Ian had deliberately let her believe she was cooking only for the three of them, if he had known all along what he was letting her in for, then he would certainly get a piece of her mind.

'I'm glad you did as you were told.'

Julie turned quickly at the sound of Cameron's voice. He had come up so quietly behind her that her senses triggered in faint alarm. 'What do you mean?' she asked with a frown.

'Your hair.'

Involuntarily she touched it, tempted to remind him again that she would have done so anyway, but deciding there was no point in provoking further antagonism. This was a very small community—and would be smaller still far too soon! It was best that they maintain some sort of halfway decent relationship.

He looked at her appraisingly and insolently, not missing one inch of her body, starting at the tips of her toes and working his way slowly upwards, pausing to rest on the pert thrust of her breasts before finally meeting her furious hazel eyes.

'You're too damned beautiful,' he growled, and it wasn't a compliment. 'I'm not sure that it was a good idea after all; you could prove an unfortunate distraction.'

Julie knew he wasn't talking about himself. In the short time she had spent in Cameron's company she had got the impression that he was always in control, always in complete charge of his life, and that no woman, however attractive, would be allowed to intrude.

'I'm sorry we did not meet when I was in England recently,' he added.

'Because then you wouldn't have insisted that I accompany Ian, is that it?' she asked crisply. 'I think you're being very insulting, Mr Storm, I can assure you I do not have a roving eye. I'm not interested in other men. I'm very happy as things are.'

Before Roger she had had no steady boyfriends. After what had happened to her mother she had always sworn she would never get married. But it had happened, she had fallen in love, and had really thought she had found the ideal man—until Roger's jealously got the better of him.

He hadn't been able to bear her to even talk to another man. At first she had been flattered, thought it proved how much he loved her, but when he had accused her of having an affair, when he would not listen when she'd explained that Tod Martin was a lifelong friend of the family and had taken her out for a meal because they hadn't seen each other for over twelve months, she had ended their relationship.

He had been very acrimonious, and their argument had hurt her deeply, causing her many sleepless nights.

'Is that so?' Cameron's brows rose mockingly, as though he thought otherwise, as though he thought she would have a field day with twenty men to take her choice from. 'You're happy with Ian?'

It was the glint in his eye that did it. Why he should have this instant damning opinion of her, she did not know. 'I am, very much so,' she told him furiously.

'What have I done, Mr Storm, to deserve such offensive comments?'

He actually looked amused. 'You've done nothing—yet.'

'You're just being prepared?'

'Something like that,' he admitted, his lips quirking.

Julie lifted her chin and glared. 'You will find that I shall do nothing except my work—to the best of my ability. Is that good enough?'

'I guess it will have to be.' Their eyes met and challenged, and then, with a sudden, surprising change of subject, he said, 'Ian is just the person I need to assist me. I am currently documenting the life of the fur seals. They are becoming an endangered species, as he's probably told you?'

'Actually no,' replied Julie. 'I've no idea what sort of work you do.'

He looked suprised, and immediately launched into an explanation. 'It's El Niño which is the problem,' he told her. 'A warm current which comes at around Christmas-time. It doesn't normally have too much effect, but once every six or seven years the flow is exceptionally large; rainfall and temperatures soar and all the fish move away. Consequently its catastrophic for life that depends on the sea.'

'Such as the fur seals,' she acknowledged.

'That's right, and seabirds and marine iguanas. Most of the young die because they can't feed and it takes many years for things to get back to normal—if ever.'

He was a totally different man when he was talking about his work—gone was the mockery and the hardness. It was very evident that he genuinely cared about wildlife. She relaxed and smiled. 'You're very passionate about your work, Mr Storm.'

'It is my one and only interest in life,' he admitted, and then, with another abrupt change of subject, 'I was actually suprised to hear Ian had got married. I thought he was an equally earnest young man, intent only on furthering his career. When I first met him a couple of years ago there wasn't even a girl on the scene. He mentioned to me then about coming out here.'

Julie smiled faintly, uncomfortably. 'It did happen rather suddenly.'

'He seemed very sure that you would come with him. Did you take much persuading?' His deep blue eyes were watchful on hers and Julie shifted uneasily. The heat was getting to her; there wasn't even a breeze to counteract the sun's intensity. It was high overhead and she hadn't eaten or drunk anything since breakfast. She had flown the six hundred miles from Ecuador to the island of Baltra, and then taken the ferry here to Santa Cruz, and now she was both hungry and thirsty and didn't really want to stand talking to Cameron Storm.

'I didn't actually jump at it,' she admitted. But that had only been because of the deception. Otherwise it had come at a perfect time.

'Because you didn't want to give up your job?'

Julie shook her head. 'Actually, I'm between jobs; I was made redundant a few months ago.'

'So it was loyalty to your husband?' There was a cynical tone to his voice now.

'Of course,' she snapped.

'But you don't share his interest in ecology?'

'No. Does it matter?'

His mouth twisted. 'Not so long as you don't whinge all the time. This is hardly the place for someone who. . .'

Julie heard no more. His words receded and were lost as the heat pounded in her head. Everything began to spin, round and round, faster and faster, until finally she lost her balance.

# CHAPTER TWO

JULIE felt herself being held against a hard, masculine body by arms that were strong and supportive, and yet surprisingly gentle. She was led to a canvas chair in the shade and a glass of water pushed into her hand.

She took a long, much needed drink and immediately her glass was refilled. 'I shouldn't have kept you out in the sun,' Cameron said. 'I'm used to it; I forget. It is easy to become dehydrated. You must drink plenty of liquids and take salt tablets if necessary. We always keep a supply.'

'Thank you,' said Julie.

'Are you hungry also? When did you last eat?'

'Not since my breakfast at seven, as a matter of fact,' she told him, 'but I can easily get myself something. I'm feeling much better now.' In fact she felt normal again and stood up.

But Cameron pushed her back down, and with a wry twist of his lips said, 'I'd advise you to make the most of it. After this you'll get no help from anyone.'

He disappeared into the tent and came back with a bread roll, a chunk of cheese and an apple, and a glass of orange juice. Julie ate ravenously, though she wasn't too pleased with the fact that Cameron sat watching her.

'When did you say you expect Ian back?' she asked, taking a bite from the rosy apple.

He lifted his broad shoulders in an easy shrug. 'Some time today, as soon as he's fixed the engine, unless it's

23

not as simple as he first thought and I have to send out an engineer.'

'And this man, Raul, will he do the cooking?'

'Tonight, yes.' His blue eyes were level on hers. 'Also tomorrow, and then he's taking a break.'

She felt better now she had eaten, not half so prickly, and she grinned. 'I hope you've all got cast-iron stomachs, because I'm not promising anything.'

'Have I been landed with a woman who cannot cook?' he growled suspiciously.

'Oh, yes, I can cook,' she said, still smiling, 'but I've never done it for the multitudes before. It's the quantities that are worrying me. You'll probably have either too little or too much until I get into the swing of it.'

He did not look amused, and as soon as she had finished eating he took her to the tent where all the records were kept. There were a couple of desks, a portable typewriter sitting on one of them, filing cabinets and an odd assortment of cupboards. 'This is where you'll be working for the time being.'

Julie looked at everything critically.

'We're way behind with the notes already,' he told her. 'They're all here, handwritten, but I'd like them typed out. You can start whenever you like.'

She half suspected that he meant now. 'Has your typist taken a break as well?' she asked impishly.

He allowed himself a faint, dry smile. 'We all try to do our own, but it can be a bit chaotic. We need someone to restore order. I trust you're capable?'

'I guess I can manage,' she said. For six years she had been secretary to the managing director of a large manufacturing Company—until they had been taken over and her services were no longer required. She had always been praised for her efficiency.

'I want things brought up to date before we leave for Vulcan,' he announced, his tone crisp and businesslike.

It sounded as thought he had a lot of hard work lined up for her, thought Julie. 'I'll begin tomorrow,' she said. 'I'd like to rest now, if you don't mind.'

The truth was she needed to get away from him. He was the most physical man she had ever met. Despite his less than welcoming attitude, he still somehow managed to excite her. Even with Roger she had not felt this instant attraction. It was unreal—and fatal!

He inclined his head. 'Very well.'

After half an hour, though, Julie became restless. She was virtually hiding from Cameron Storm and that was stupid. Surely she could handle these emotions without betraying herself?

She emerged from the tent, and to her dismay he was out there, standing just a few yards away, not looking in her direction, seeming to be deep in thought, but as if he sensed her presence he turned, and their eyes met for a brief, tension-packed second.

'I thought I'd take a walk into Puerto Ayora,' she said, pasting a brilliant smile to her lips. 'I shan't have much time for shopping once I start work, and there are a couple of things I might need. Is it far?'

'Too far to walk,' he growled.

'Then perhaps I could borrow the Jeep?' she asked brightly.

But her smile didn't charm him. Instead, he scowled ferociously and rasped, 'The last thing I want is you getting lost. I'd better take you.'

It was clear he was offering out of a sense of duty, but Julie wanted to get away from him, not spend more time together. One of the reasons she had come out here was to get over a broken heart, not find herself attracted to someone else. It was a disaster waiting to happen and she had to stop it right here and now. 'That's not necessary,' she protested firmly, 'I'll be perfectly all right by myself.'

But Cameron was insistent. 'I happen to think it is. Come, let us go.'

His tone was sharp, and unhappily she dodged back into the tent for her bag before climbing into the Jeep beside him. To her consternation she felt his presence even more strongly than before, something invisible and intangible pulling her towards him. It caused an alien tightening in the pit of her stomach, a fractional quickening of her pulses. Even the masculine smell of him was like an aphrodisiac.

'I don't know what you are expecting to buy in Puerto Ayora.' His deep voice broke the spell. 'There are shops there, yes, but it's not a busy cosmopolitan town.' It was almost an accusation, as though he thought her only interest would be in expensive perfumes and designer clothes. Her fault, she supposed, for turning up in something that was far more suited to Paris then the beach.

'I realise that,' she said lightly, 'but I thought I'd get some more sun-block, just in case.' Although her hair was dark her skin was suprisingly fair. 'I'm sure you wouldn't like it if I got sunburnt and was unable to work.'

Her attempt at humour failed. 'You're absolutely right,' he snarled.

'And I presume there are no shops where we're going?'

He gave a snarl of humourless laughter. 'Vulcan is not even inhabited.'

Meaning it would be just the three of them; completely, totally alone! The thought sent a further shiver of apprehension down Julie's spine.

The houses in Puerto Ayora were all flat-roofed and single-storeyed, well-built and painted either deep pink or white, although most of them looked as though they could do with another coat of paint. Conversely, there were the odd one or two quite pretty houses, well looked after, with lawns, and various shrubs and trees that were definitely not endemic to the islands.

There were actually all sorts of shops, far more than she had anticipated, selling everything from essential foodstuffs to cheap souvenirs. Cameron stopped outside one and picked up a straw hat which he perched on top of her head. 'You'd better take that,' he said drily.

Julie looked at herself in the tiny mirror provided and burst out laughing. 'I don't think so.' But she tried on another, and even Cameron agreed it suited her much better.

She would have liked to linger longer, but sensed his impatience once her purchases were made, and it was really no fun in the circumstances. Why he was trailing around after her, she did not know. Why couldn't he have stayed in the Jeep? Except that Cameron Storm did not strike her as the type of man who would sit around waiting for a woman.

Back in the vehicle, she again felt the pull of his powerful magnetism, but did not realise she was in grave danger of giving herself away until he told her to relax.

'You're sitting there with your hands clenched, looking as though you're ready to do battle.'

'I'm just not used to bumping around in a Jeep,' she

improvised quickly. He was again driving as though there were no tomorrow.

His lips twisted, as if he found her explanation less than credible, and she expected some further caustic comment. Surprisingly, though, he remained silent for the rest of the journey.

To her relief, Ian had returned in their absence. He came to meet her, pulling her into his arms, giving, she thought, a very creditable show of having greatly missed his supposed wife.

Julie squinted at Cameron over Ian's shoulder and saw him watching them closely, a deeply disturbing frown on his face. Wasn't Ian's performance convincing enough? She felt a quiver of unease, and once in the tent that they were to share Julie voiced her misgivings. 'I have a feeling he knows.'

'How can he?' Ian asked fiercely. 'It's all in your mind.'

'He was watching us like a hawk.'

'You've not said anything to make him suspicious?'

'No. Have you? He said some mighty funny things when we first met.'

'Of course not,' Ian assured her. 'What do you take me for, a fool? I want this job more than anything in the world. You're just jumpy, that's all. Once you've settled in everything will be fine.'

They were sitting facing each other on the edge of their camp-beds and she looked at him urgently. 'Neither did he insist you bring me for the reason you thought.'

Ian frowned.

'It's not because he's wary of single girls, it's because he didn't want to split us up for so long.'

'Is that what he said?' queried Ian sharply.

'Yes.'

'Are you sure?'

'Of course I'm sure.'

He shook his head, mystified. 'I don't see how I could have made such a mistake. He quite clearly stated that he preferred a married woman in the camp.'

'So what are we going to do?' she asked, twisting the ring on her finger. 'Are we going to tell him?'

Ian shook his head. 'Most definitely not. He's a very straight man who hates deceit. He could easily send us both home for obtaining work under false pretences. I think we should sit tight and say nothing.'

Julie was not so sure; she really did think honesty would be best policy. 'He might not send us back,' she said pleadingly.

'I can't take the risk,' answered Ian. 'Besides, even if he didn't send us home I'd be worried to death about you.'

Julie frowned. 'What do you mean?'

'The guys here are a nice enough bunch, but I've heard a few moans about there being no available women. Wearing a wedding-ring will be your best protection. After Roger I don't think you'd be happy having to fight off further advances.'

'Perish the thought,' she said strongly. 'I'm off men forever.' Which was why her reaction to Cameron was all the more amazing. It was definitely something she had to fight and she had no intention of telling her twin about it.

'So we'll carry on as we are?'

She nodded, and Ian leapt across and pulled her into his arms. 'Thank you, Sis. Thank you.' There was a bond between them that was much stronger than that between ordinary brothers and sisters, and when she thought back to all his heartache, to his months of unhappiness, and the change in him when this trip was planned, this was the least she could do.

It was such a little deceit, it couldn't possibly hurt anyone, and if he was right about the men complaining about their enforced celibacy, then being *Mrs* Drummond was exactly what she needed.

'I'm sorry to break up such a tender little reunion, but there's work to be done out here.' Cameron Storm's caustic voice cut into her thoughts. Through the opening of the tent he could see them quite clearly.

Julie pulled out of her brother's arms. 'He's all yours.'

And Ian stood up and looked guilty. 'I'm sorry, Cameron, it's just that——'

'I know, I know, you haven't seen each other for over a week,' he responded curtly, 'but there'll be plenty of time for that later. I want to see your records. I want to discuss your findings on Pinzón yesterday.'

His tone seemed unnecessarily sharp, thought Julie, but she was glad he had seen her and Ian together.

She looked longingly again at the sea, at the white sandy beach shelving gently down to it. Cameron and her brother were deep in conversation some yards away, she needn't feel fearful now of him watching her.

Her mind made up, Julie slipped out of her clothes and into her bikini—cream and deep red stripes, bought especially to come out here, when she had thought she would be doing plenty of sunbathing! It enhanced her curves, revealed the flatness of her stomach and the slenderness of her hips. But she had been mistaken in thinking that she could take a swim unnoticed. As she ran lightly across the sand two pairs of eyes swivelled in her direction.

The water, inviting though it looked, was so icy-cold it took her breath away, but because she was being watched Julie pretended not to be affected. She was a strong swimmer and swam a hundred yards or more away from the beach before stopping and floating on her back.

By now she had got used to the temperature, although it was still too cold to stay in for very long. The sun warmed her upturned face and the sky was a very deep azure. She looked back at the beach, dotted with its brown tents. It was backed by volcanic rock and the occasional shrub.

A little further out Julie thought she saw the shape of a fin cutting through the water, and had a sudden mental image of being eaten by a shark. It was enough to panic her into returning to shore as quickly as her arms and legs would take her, and when she got there Cameron Storm was waiting.

'I saw a shark,' she panted. 'Why didn't you warn me?'

To her amazement he smiled, even though a trifle grimly.

'There are sharks in these waters, yes,' he announced matter-of-factly, 'but no one has ever been attacked. There are too many fish for them to be interested in humans, though I would recommend leaving the water if you cut or graze yourself.'

Julie was not convinced. There was always a first time.

'Have you no other swimwear?'

His brusque question took her by surprise. 'Well, yes, but why?'

'Because wearing something as skimpy as that in front of a group of men who haven't seen a woman in months is asking for trouble.'

Although he was confirming Ian's fears, Julie deeply resented his attitude. 'Is it really me you're concerned for?' she asked fiercely. 'Or the fact that your team might have their mind taken off their work?' He had no right dictating like this. First of all her hair, now her bikini—what next would he complain about?

'Both,' he snarled.

Her hazel eyes were steady on his. 'Since there's no one about at this moment I cannot see what your problem is, Mr Storm. Are you sure it's not *your* blood pressure that's rising?' It was unwise to speak to him like this, she knew, but he was being impossible.

Cameron completely ignored her question. 'So long as you restrict your swimming activities to when there is no one else about I shall say no more.'

Their eyes met, his hard and unreadable, with no indication what real thoughts were going through his mind. She maintained the contact for several seconds, then with a toss of her head she turned and walked away.

Thankfully Ian was not in the tent, so she was able to towel herself dry and pull her T-shirt and shorts back on. She rubbed most of the moisture out of her hair and then scraped it severely back in a ponytail.

By now Raul had arrived to begin preparations for the evening meal. The tawny-skinned local boy did not speak any English but he had a permanent smile and whistled softly to himself as he worked. Rather than stand and watch, Julie helped scrub endless potatoes, which were put in the ovens to be baked in their jackets, she filleted fish and laid the long trestle-tables where everyone ate.

And when all that was done she went looking for Ian. She found him in the 'office', busy scribbling notes. He looked up and smiled. 'Did you enjoy your swim?'

'Until Cameron Storm told me off.'

'For what?' he asked with a frown.

'Wearing a bikini. I might tempt the other men, he said. What the hell does he think I am? A sex siren?'

A deep voice came from behind. 'I think you don't know the power of your beautiful body.'

She whirled and met the mocking force of blue eyes.

'I don't think you realise the danger you could be putting yourself in,' he said quietly, and then to Ian, 'Your *wife* is too beautiful for her own good. I congratulate you, but I hadn't foreseen it could be a problem.'

'If I'm a problem to you I'll go back home,' Julie retorted at once, wondering if Ian had noticed his emphasis on the word wife, or whether she was imagining it because of her unease over the situation.

A muscle jerked in the big man's jaw. 'That won't be necessary.'

And Ian added a frantic plea. 'Of course not, Julie, it's just a matter of being sensible. I'm proud of you, but I wouldn't like it either if I thought the rest of the team were ogling you.' His eyes pleaded with her to calm down.

But she hated him siding with Cameron, even though she knew he was right. 'I'm to make myself as unattractive as possible, is that what you're saying?'

Ian looked appalled, and it was clear he felt that she was putting his job in jeopardy. Cameron, on the other hand, laughed. 'What a spitfire you've chosen for yourself, Ian. I'll leave you to deal with her.'

When he had gone Ian looked at Julie worriedly. 'How could you speak to Cameron Storm like that? Don't you realise you could be jeopardising my whole future?'

She shook her head in angry frustration. 'He just rubs me up the wrong way.'

'Please,' he pleaded, 'try to get on with him, even if you don't like him. For *my* sake.'

But Julie was still in high dudgeon. 'I'll try, but it will be mighty impossible. If he thinks he can dictate to me then he's mistaken.' And so saying, she flounced out of the tent.

To her dismay Cameron was standing right outside; she almost cannoned into him, would have done so if he hadn't put out an arm to stop her. 'What's the rush?' There was still a quirk to his lips, a faint light of amusement in his eyes.

She shook herself free, but not before she felt a dangerous tingle of electricity. 'No rush,' she told him, trying her hardest to maintain some degreee of dignity. After her disastrous affair with Roger she could not understand how or why this was happening. It revealed a vulnerability she hadn't expected, and it was this very defencelessness that was making her snappy.

'Are you saying that you always charge around like a bull in a china shop?'

Julie's eyes flashed. 'Only when I'm angry.'

Cameron Storm had generous bushy brows and they rose now, his deep blue thickly fringed eyes intent on her face. 'You don't take kindly to being told what to do, do you?'

'Not when I think it's unnecessary.' She held his

gaze, stood that little bit straighter, her chin defiantly high.

'It's for your own good—for your own protection, in fact.'

Aware that Ian could hear every word, Julie knew she had to be careful. 'But I'm not a fool,' she insisted. 'I am aware that there are certain bounds of decency when there's one woman among several men. You can be assured I will conduct myself with absolute decorum.'

His eyes held hers for several more long, spine-tingling seconds. 'That is good to hear.'

Julie was the first to look away. She felt like scooting back to her tent, wanting time to free herself of these anguished feelings; instead she strolled unhurriedly towards the kitchen to see how Raul was getting on.

By the time the first of the men began to filter back the meal was almost ready. Ian introduced her to each one in turn, and judging by their admiring looks Julie could well understand both his and Cameron's concern.

They were a mixed bunch, ranging in age from early twenties to mid-fifties. Cameron was the definite leader, although, to give him his due, he did not act as the big chief. He was at one with the men and they got on well together. It was easy to understand his misgivings when she had suddenly appeared in their midst.

Julie had never really thought of herself as being beautiful. She had good bone-structure, yes, but she had always considered her face pretty ordinary, her eyes a little too small, her mouth a little too wide. Her hair was her best feature. Thick and black and glossy, she wore it without a fringe, normally falling in a cascade of luxuriant waves down her back. Now, of course, it was scraped tightly and unbecomingly back and confined in a band.

As they sat down to eat she was aware of Cameron's eyes on her. He was diagonally opposite, with Ian on her right and a blond giant of a man, who had been introduced as Jake, on her left. 'Jake hails from Australia and he's an expert on lichens.' Ian informed her.

'I'm afraid I don't know anything about them,' Julie apologised.

Jake laughed. 'I guesss you'll learn all sorts of things by the time you've finished typing our notes.'

'I expect so,' Julie acknowledged.

'Ian's lucky you were able to come with him.'

'Are you married yourself?' asked Julie. Jake was nearer forty than thirty, probably much the same age as Cameron, with a good body and blue eyes too, although they were nowhere near as deep and powerful.

She felt Cameron's eyes on her again now, and it was almost as though he was warning her not to get too friendly, which was ridiculous. What was she supposed to do—talk to no one? Or was it her imagination? Was she imagining criticism when none was there?

'I was,' the man admitted with a wry smile. 'It didn't work out. Maggie objected to the fact that I spent so much time away. It's wrong to marry someone who's in a completely different job; they simply don't understand.'

'So no one here is married?' she asked.

'No, that's not right,' he replied. 'Ray over there is.' He nodded towards the oldest of the team. 'But his wife doesn't mind him being away. She runs her own business and has plenty to do. And Sim, he's married.

He could have brought his wife, she's a biologist as well, but she's working on another project, and then there's young Andy, he's only been married six months.'

Julie frowned. So why hadn't Cameron suggested this boy bring his wife as well? Unless, of course, she had no skills that were necessary to their research; Cameron wouldn't want to carry dead weight. 'What does Andy's wife do?' she asked.

'She's a nurse, I believe,' Jake answered, 'working on a cruise liner. It's where they met. They're used to spending time apart. He reckons it's more than worthwhile when they do get together.'

'Do you miss not having a woman in your life?'

'Hell, yes, sometimes.' His eyes twinkled at her. 'It's going to be refreshing having you here.'

'Don't get any ideas,' she warned him, though she smiled as she spoke. 'Ian packs quite a punch.'

'Just joshing,' he said. 'I wouldn't jeopardise my job. This is an ongoing project—biologists come and go, some don't stay long, some for years. Cameron loves the place.'

They both looked across the table as they spoke and Cameron's eyes were upon them, narrowed and assessing, though he smiled and acknowledged Jake.

'I was just telling Julie how much I enjoy my work here,' said the Australian, seeing nothing wrong in Cameron's expression.

'It would be unprofitable if you didn't,' agreed Cameron drily. 'We can only hope that *Mrs* Drummond enjoys her work too.'

The emphasis on her marital status this time, she decided, was a warning to Jake that she was a married woman. She turned to Ian at her other side, and he smiled warmly and touched her hand. 'All right?' he asked quietly.

She nodded, and tried to concentrate on her meal, but it was difficult with Cameron sitting so near. She was relieved when it was all over, when she was able to help Raul clear away and wash up.

By this time it was dark, no long twilight like in England, but a rapid descent of the sun and then total darkness. It was still only a little after seven.

Solar lamps, that had been sitting in the sun all day gathering energy, were switched on and the whole camp looked festive. The men sat around in groups talking and Julie found herself alone with Ian and Cameron. It had been a long day, though, and she felt tired, and after an hour listening to the two men talk shop, trying to ignore the fact that her body was responding to Cameron's in a way that made her feel uncomfortable, she yawned and stretched, and declared that she was going to bed.

Ian dutifully gave her a kiss on the cheek. 'You poor darling, you've had a tiring day. I'll try not to wake you when I turn in.'

She smiled. 'Goodnight, Ian.' And then she turned to Cameron and bade him goodnight too.

Their eyes met and held briefly. 'Goodnight, Julie.'

But she did not sleep, she was far too aware of this man who had made such an impact on her life in such a short space of time. She could only be thankful that there were no reciprocal feelings; that would have been hell. There was no way then that she could have gone on with this charade.

When Ian came to bed a couple of hours later she pretended to be asleep. Almost within minutes his breathing deepened; he was happy here, there was absolutely nothing on his conscience to keep him awake.

Julie tossed and turned and in the end decided to get some fresh air. It was noticeably cooler now and she pulled a cardigan about her shoulders. There were no lights, every tent was in darkness; she felt quite safe.

She walked down to the shore and stood listening to the lap of the waves, watching the pattern of reflections from a full, silvery moon, totally unprepared when a harsh voice came out of the darkness.

'Mrs Drummond, what the hell do you think you are doing?'

# CHAPTER THREE

JULIE had heard no movement behind her; Cameron had approached with all the stealth of a tiger. She swung around, her heart hammering unsteadily in her breast. 'I'm not doing anything.'

'It looks to me as though you're asking for trouble,' he growled.

She frowned. 'What do you mean?' He was still wearing the same shirt and trousers as earlier, though whether he had pulled them on again when he saw her, or whether he had not yet gone to bed, Julie had no idea. She did not even know what time it was.

Cameron's eyes glittered. 'I'm sure you're not unaware that the moon shining on you renders your nightdress virtually transparent. And that knitted thing doesn't hide much.'

Julie's heart went into panic. How long had he stood watching her before making his presence known? And how much could he see? 'I couldn't sleep,' she retorted defensively, clutching the cardigan tightly around her throat as if by so doing it gave her some form of protection.

'It cannot have escaped your notice that most of the tents are open-sided. If any of the men are awake they will not have failed to see you out here.'

And he thought she was doing it deliberately! Her chin came up. 'Then they will not have *failed* to see that you followed me. What do you think they will

40

make of that?' And why was his opinion of her so very, very low?

The chiselled planes of his face grew harder and more angular; his mouth tightened. 'If they have assessed the situation correctly they will know I have come to warn you.' His voice was dangerously low, a threatening growl that shivered across Julie's cruelly exposed nerve-endings.

She held the neck of her cardigan with both hands, her arms pressed close to her sides.

'You have been here less than twelve hours, Mrs Drummond,' he went on, 'and already you are becoming a nuisance.'

His constant formality unnerved her. Despite Ian's confidence, she felt sure Cameron suspected all was not as it should be. He watched them too closely, too often, and always there was calculation in his eyes. Why he should be suspicious, she did not know, but she was sure he was.

He moved so that his back was to the moon instead of hers, and she imagined it was to see her face more clearly, put her at an even bigger disadvantage.

She gave a tiny laugh, recalling Ian's plea that she try to get on with his boss. 'Why is it that I cannot seem to do anything right?'

Brows lifted. 'Surely it's a matter of basic intelligence?'

'Haven't you ever had women working here before?'

He inclined his head. 'Yes, we've had female scientists.'

'And were you as much on their backs as you are mine?'

His mouth twisted. 'It wasn't necessary. For one thing they did not flaunt themselves.'

'Flaunt?' echoed Julie, all her good intentions fading. 'Is that what you think I'm doing? Heavens, Mr Storm, you're seeing things that are not there.'

'I don't think so,' he answered. 'No woman can be as subliminally unaware of what she is doing as you're suggesting.'

Julie shook her head violently, her hair, which she had taken out of its pins when she went to bed, falling forward over her face. 'What's the point in trying to defend myself,' she asked crossly, 'when you'll believe only what you want to believe? I'm going back to bed.'

But before she had even turned he reached out, and to her utter amazement began stroking back the hair from her face. 'Your hair looks blue in the moonlight,' he muttered. 'It has the gloss of a raven's wing.'

So had his, she thought. It was odd that her hair should be the same colour as Cameron's, whereas her twin's was so much lighter. He seemed mesmerised by it, and when his fingers accidentally brushed her cheek Julie felt as though a thousand volts of electricity had shot through her.

At exactly the same instant Cameron withdrew, as though he had felt her reaction—or as though he had been testing her! Was this what it was all about? Was this why he had joined her, why he had touched her? Was he checking her loyalty to Ian?

Julie's heart thudded fit to burst and she looked into his eyes with something approaching panic, praying with all her heart that he hadn't sensed her reaction. It seemed forever that they held each other's gaze, even though it could have been for no more than a fraction of a second. Then with a cry like a startled bird Julie raced back to her tent.

'Julie!' Cameron's low voice came to her in the

velvety softness of the night, but she ignored it. Whatever he had to say could only be to her shame, to her detriment. She had been in very grave danger of giving herself away, of putting Ian's job at risk.

Upon reaching the tent, she dived inside and threw herself down on the bed. Her heart pounded so loudly that it echoed in her ears, her pulses raced and every limb trembled. And all because of one man! All because Cameron Storm had touched her! It didn't bear thinking about.

'Where have you been?' Ian's gruff, sleepy voice startled her.

'Did I wake you? I'm sorry. I—I couldn't sleep so I went for a walk.' She tried desperately to control her breathing.

'Oh.' He seemed satisfied, turned over, and was asleep again within seconds.

It seemed an aeon before Julie finally drifted into sleep, her mind tormented, her very sanity threatened. She must never let herself get into such a volatile situation again. She even began to wonder whether it had been her imagination that Cameron had touched her and sparked off this reaction. Whatever, he was a dangerous man, and she had to steer clear of him.

Ian was awake and dressed before Julie even stirred. He touched her shoulder. 'Time to get up, Sis.'

Her eyes shot wide instantly.

'You're supposed to be helping with cooking breakfast, and there are packed lunches to be put up. If you don't want to incur Cameron's wrath again you'd better get moving.'

Mention of her protagonist's name was enough to galvanise Julie into action, and by the time the rest of the team put in an appearance the trestle-tables were laid, sausages and eggs cooked, bread sliced, tea and coffee made. All with Raul's help, of course. His indefatigable cheerfulness had helped restore her equilibrium.

She did not sit down with them this morning, instead remaining in the kitchen making sandwiches. The sides of the tent, which were rolled down when it wasn't in use because, she had been told, mocking-birds or even sea-lions came to steal food, were up out of the way and she could see Cameron sitting at the table with the other men.

Jake came across to wish her a cheerful good morning. 'You sure are a sight for sore eyes.'

She gave him a warm smile. 'Thank you, kind sir.' His friendliness was like balm to her unsettled thoughts.

'I hear you'll be leaving for Vulcan soon, that's a pity. I shall miss you. You're the best thing that's happened to us for a long time.'

'You're an old flatterer,' she said, but she appreciated his compliment all the same.

He stayed talking for several more minutes before going to his seat and Julie was taken completely by surprise when Cameron suddenly appeared at her side. 'Are you encouraging Jake?' he asked harshly.

The question was so unexpected that her mouth fell open. 'Of course not.'

'He seems mighty friendly.'

'And why shouldn't he be?' she asked. 'Am I supposed to speak to no one but you and Ian?'

'I don't want you giving them the wrong impression.'

She frowned. 'And that is?'

'That the bit of gold on your finger makes no difference.'

'How dare you?' Julie was sorely tempted to raise her hand to his cheek, except that it would have the unfortunate effect of attracting everyone's attention, and she wanted to avoid that at all costs. This battle between her and Cameron was personal.

'Just make sure that you watch what you're doing,' he growled. 'And why aren't you eating with the rest of us?'

'Because I need to finish the lunches,' she said quietly.

He frowned as he looked at the shadows beneath her eyes. 'If you refrained from midnight walks you might be able to get up in time to organise yourself.'

Julie felt the reproof was unfounded. 'I only walked because I couldn't sleep, but you need never fear that my work will suffer because of it.'

'It had better not.'

His tone seemed unnecessarily sharp and she guessed that it was really because of Jake. They had laughed a lot and he must have compared it with their own, often aggressive relationship. No other man had ever stirred her like this, and she could only suppose it was fear of being found out that put her on the defensive—and also the very real emotions he managed to evoke in her.

After breakfast, Ian asked what Cameron had said. 'I thought he looked a bit uptight.'

She shrugged. 'He was checking that I can cope, that's all.' Best not to tell her brother about their unfortunate meeting last night, or his accusations regarding Jake.

Ian's frown changed to a smile. 'He's a real nice guy

when you get to know him. He's always concerned about his fellow men.'

Julie's smile was much weaker than her twin's. 'I'll reserve judgement.'

'You'll learn to like him,' said Ian confidently. 'Everyone does. No one's ever said a bad word against him.'

The men began to drift away, until finally there was only Cameron left. A dreadful feeling began to settle in the pit of Julie's stomach. Even Raul had gone back to his village; she was completely alone, completely at his mercy. 'Aren't you joining your men?' she asked, trying to keep her tone light and cheerful.

'There are things I need to explain.'

'Typing out notes doesn't need any explanations.' She felt sure he was using this as an excuse to antagonise her further.

'There are other matters.'

He had already opened the sides of the tent until there was no more than a roof and they stepped beneath it now and Julie sat down at the desk. Regardless of its open sides, Cameron still seemed to fill the area with his presence, her awareness of him so powerful that she knew it would be impossible to concentrate on any single task until he left her alone.

He indicated an untidy pile of handwritten notes—a huge pile! 'These all belong to the various members of the team; I trust you'll be able to read their writing.'

Julie said nothing.

'And this, here, is my work. I've kept my own field-study notes reasonably up to date, as you can see. But I seem to have got way behind with the book I am writing.'

'Book?' This did surprise Julie. Nothing had been said about a book.

'Perhaps I forgot to mention it,' he announced lazily.

Or perhaps it had been deliberate! Perhaps he hadn't wanted her to know exactly how much work was involved; perhaps he had thought it would scare her away! And he desperately needed a typist, that much was very evident. 'What is it about?' she asked curiously.

'What else but these islands?' Again his whole demeanour changed, his eyes lighting with pleasure in the work he was doing. 'There have been dozens of books written about the unique wildlife found here— I've written several myself, each one specialising in a different subject. This one is dedicated to my dear friends, the fur seals.'

'It's just about them, nothing else?' she asked in amazement. How much could be written about such animals?

'Just the fur seals,' he agreed, the harsh angles of his face softened by a caring smile.

Julie wondered what it would feel like to have him smile at her like that? Best not to know. It could be devastating.

'Apart from the catastrophic effects of El Niño,' he continued, 'they were brought dangerously nearly to extinction in the eighteen hundreds. One fur seal hunter boasted of killing five thousand seals in two months. Can you believe that?' There was anger now, fury at the thoughtless acts of these men.

He showed her drawings too, and Julie looked at them in amazement. 'These are good. Did you do them?'

He inclined his head in acknowledgement.

'You're very talented.'

He lifted his shoulders modestly. 'As you can see, there is a lot of typing to be done; everything is behind, and I have a five-week deadline for my book. I still have the last chapter to finish, but that won't take long.'

'You certainly intend to keep me busy.'

Well-marked brows rose. 'Isn't that what you're here for?'

'Well, yes,' he said, 'but I did think I'd have some time to myself.' And how she wished that she had not been so eager to sit down—it put her at a definite disadvantage.

Towering arrogantly over her, Cameron looked cool and comfortable, whereas she already felt a slight sheen of perspiration. The muskiness of his skin assailed her nostrils and she felt his essential maleness. Every nerve-end began to quiver. She even began to wonder what his body was like beneath the thin cotton of his shirt.

He grinned, showing his very even white teeth. 'So that's it. You thought it would be one big holiday. That you could laze around and swim and sunbathe and generally have a good time.' His smile went as suddenly as it had appeared. 'I'm sorry to disappoint you but everyone here pulls their weight—and that includes you.'

Determined not to let him get to her, she gave him one of her warmest smiles. 'I would never dream of doing otherwise, Mr Storm.'

He held her gaze, clearly not sure whether she was being genuine or sarcastic. 'I'm glad you understand. I suggest you make a start. If you want me just shout; I'll be around somewhere.'

'You mean, you're not joining the others?'

'You sound disappointed.'

She shrugged carelessly. 'It doesn't matter to me. I just get the feeling you don't think I can cope.'

His full lips pulled down at the corners. 'I would be a fool to leave you here until I am sure.'

'Perhaps I should have brought proof of my qualifications, and a letter of reference from my last employer?' she asked, still keeping her tone deliberately cheerful. 'I can assure you I am extremely capable.'

'And very beautiful as well.'

Julie had not expected this and it was her turn to look suspicious. 'I wonder why you think it necessary to keep telling me that?'

His brows, as dark as hers but much thicker and heavier, rose enquiringly. 'Do we have a woman who doesn't like compliments?'

'Not if that's what it was,' she replied, 'but it sounded more like an accusation. You seem to think I'm conscious of the way I look and use it to my advantage.'

'And don't you?' Again their eyes locked into each other's, his mocking, hers wary.

She knew he was thinking of Jake, but in actual fact the Australian was well out of mind. Ian had warned her how dangerously attractive Cameron was, but she had never thought she would succumb so instantly. 'No, I do not,' she said, and was appalled to hear a tremor in her voice.

'I suppose you're going to tell me next that you're a happily married woman and love Ian to distraction?'

Warning bells rang. It was not so much what he said but the way that he said it. Or was she imagining things? 'Of course I love Ian.' And this, at least, was the truth.

'I think you'd better get started,' he said gruffly, and walked out of the tent.

It was difficult to give full attention to the task in front of her. Images of Cameron Storm kept feeding themselves into her mind's eye; she was too aware of him, too aware of his male magnetism, too aware of the profound effect he was having on her, and too worried by the fact that he seemed to know they were masquerading. She typed automatically, without fully comprehending the written words. Several times she tore the paper out of the machine and started again.

When he came back a short time later he looked accusingly at the growing pile of discarded sheets in the waste-bin. 'Was Ian telling lies?'

'Not at all,' she replied firmly. 'I had to get used to the typewriter.' It was the best excuse she could think of.

'Only a bad workman blames his tools,' he reminded her, eyes narrowed thoughtfully. 'Perhaps there's something else bothering you?'

'Nothing at all,' she lied, looking steadily into his eyes. Lord, they were beautiful. She had never seen eyes of such a deep, intense blue. They were hypnotic; she could feel herself being transfixed by them—she almost felt that it was possible to drown in them.

'You seem nervous in my presence—as though you have something to hide?' His white teeth were exposed in a dangerous smile.

Julie felt panic but managed a laugh. 'What could I possibly have to hide? You're imagining things. Maybe I'm a little nervous about whether I can cope with the heat, but that is all.'

'Nervous—about the heat?' he questioned caustically. 'A very odd fear. Are you sure it's not something else?'

'Of course not,' she answered, and was shocked to hear a tremor in her voice.

He looked at her long and hard, eyes narrowed, and Julie wasn't sure how she managed to keep her nerve.

'In that case,' he said finally, a knowing twist to his lips, 'you won't object if I work here also.' He sat down at the other desk, picked up a pencil and began scribbling in a notebook.

Julie realised it was imperative now that she get everything right, that she did not draw attention to herself by wasting more paper and more time by making stupid mistakes. She made herself channel her vision on to the pieces of paper on her desk, refusing to let her eyes stray in Cameron's direction.

Fortunately she was not facing him and it worked— for a short time. But all too soon she found herself glancing sideways in his direction. To her amazement he was watching her, his pencil tapping on a thumbnail, his eyes enigmatic. She had thought he was intent on his writing, had never dreamt that his attention had been diverted too.

She felt her heart begin a stampede all of its own, and without even acknowledging him she dragged her eyes back to her work. For the next hour she typed non-stop, until her neck and shoulders ached and every nerve in her body screamed out for mercy.

'I think you deserve a break.'

Julie wondered how long Cameron had been watching her this time. 'I must admit I am a bit stiff.' She rubbed her hand across the back of her neck and rotated her head in an effort to relieve some of the tension.

He pushed himself up and moved with casual intention behind her. 'Here, let me.'

It was totally unexpected, and the feel of his powerful hands on the back of her neck made Julie grow even more tense. Every muscle in her body locked.

'Relax,' he murmured soothingly.

'Please, it doesn't matter. I'll be all right.' Even to her own ears she sounded breathless. What must he be thinking?

'No, you won't. Goodness, you're knotted.' His fingers manipulated and massaged, thumbs probing, fingers sliding over the arch of her collarbone, up the sides of her neck, finding instinctively the troublesome spots.

Julie realised the futility of trying to stop him—nor could she stop the fury of feelings that exploded inside her. Although she knew it was an act of concern, something he would do for anyone in the same situation, it nevertheless triggered emotions she would far rather ignore.

'That's better,' he growled, as he felt some of the stiffness ease out of her. 'Does it feel good?'

God, how could she answer such a question intelligently? It felt like heaven. She let her head drop back on her shoulders, her eyes closed because she did not want to acknowledge that it was Cameron Storm doing this to her. It was sheer bliss. She conceded with a tiny, 'Mmm,' of satisfaction. 'You certainly know what you're doing.'

Her nerve-ends were quivering and dangerously sensitive, and Julie knew she was in grave danger of giving herself away. Her mouth had never felt so dry, and she licked her lips and swallowed hard, and all the time Cameron assaulted her senses.

He pushed the thin straps of her sun-top out of the way and she stiffened fractionally, but all he did was massage her shoulders. And just when Julie felt she could stand it no longer, when every pulse in her body screamed in protest, when her heartbeats were all out of order, he abruptly stopped. 'I think that should do.'

His voice sounded grim, and there was a tautness to his face that had not been there before. Julie wondered in horror whether he had somehow guessed her reaction. And if that was so. . . She came crashing down to earth. It did not bear thinking about. 'Thank you,' she stammered, pushing herself to her feet. 'I think I'll get a drink.' And she almost ran out of the tent.

She found herself gasping for air, her heart hammering, her breasts rising and falling, her whole body bathed in a sheen of perspiration. She poured herself a beaker of water and drank thirstily, and then another, and she was halfway through that one when Cameron joined her.

There was nothing now on his face to register that he had sensed her reaction to him. He had obviously decided to ignore it, and for this she was grateful. She gave him a weak smile. 'Would you like some?'

The water was delivered to their camp on a regular basis, so that there was always a fresh supply for drinking and cooking purposes. Their clothes and themselves were washed in sea-water with special soap, and Ian had assured her that she would soon get used to it.

'Yes, please.' His tone was gruffer than normal.

Julie did not look at him as she filled another beaker,

pushing it into his hand and then walking a few steps away to stare out at the turquoise waters of the Pacific Ocean. Her heartbeats had returned to normal but she was still far too aware of Cameron Storm for her own good.

'We could go for a swim,' came his surprising suggestion.

'What a wonderful idea.' It was the perfect antidote for her overheated body. Just the thought of it cheered her up. She turned to him with a sudden challenging smile. 'I bet I'm ready before you.'

She put down her empty beaker and ran over to her tent, changing swiftly into the cream and red bikini, but Cameron was quicker. He was waiting for her—magnificently male in a pair of brief black swimming-trunks, silky dark hair shadowing the dangerous shape of him, legs long and lean, stomach hard and flat. In one hand he held a couple of masks. 'I thought we'd go snorkelling. Ever done it?'

The crisis was over, she thought in relief. Obviously the answer was to keep the atmosphere light. 'No, I haven't,' she admitted.

'It's a must out here,' he told her. 'There is so much to see.'

And so they waded into the sea, Julie prepared this time for the lower temperature of the water, though it did not stop her shivering. 'Why is it cold when it's so hot on land?' she asked.

'Everyone asks that,' he said with a smile. 'It's because of the cool Humboldt current which sweeps up from Antarctica. That's why we have penguins. They're normally only associated with the colder regions of the southern hemisphere, but because of this current they're able to live here. The Galapagos penguin is the most northerly in the world.'

'Will I see any?' she asked, intrigued.

'Without a doubt. They're not on all of the islands, of course. A lot of wildlife and plantlife is peculiar to one island only. It's what makes the whole place so fascinating.' Again his face lit up as he spoke, and Julie could not help feeling some of his enthusiasm.

By now they were ready to strike out. They fixed their masks and snorkels in place and, swimming face down in the water, Julie was amazed at the colour and variety of sea-life; starfish and anemones put on an exotic display, and schools of brilliantly coloured fish darted beneath them. Everything was new and wonderful and totally breathtaking.

And then, unbelievably, after they had been swimming for almost twenty minutes, and Julie was on the verge of suggesting they go back because she was desperately cold, a baby sea-lion came and stared at her. It was beyond belief and Julie turned to Cameron in delight. His eyes smiled through his mask, and shortly after that they returned to shore.

Julie was shivering but happy. 'That was, without a doubt, the most incredible experience of my life,' she said, throwing herself down on the hot sand. 'I've never seen anything like it.'

'It's only the tip of the iceberg,' he told her. 'Wildlife here is fearless of man. You will see and experience a lot more that will delight you before you go back to England. Though if you want to swim for long periods at a time I would recommend a wet suit.'

He lay down beside her and Julie felt an instant tingling of her senses. She closed her eyes to try and shut him out but it was an impossibility. Cameron

Storm was larger than life; he was invading her senses, turning her world upside-down, and she did not know what she could do about it without giving away the fact that Ian was not her husband but her brother.

Already the sun had dried them. Julie was warm again, too warm, and not all of it due to the heat of the day. 'I think you ought to put on some of your sunblock.' Cameron's voice came through her haze of thought. 'Shall I fetch it for you?'

To her consternation, Julie discovered that he was watching her again. An uncomfortable prickly heat broke out on her skin. Why was he doing this? She shook her head and tried to smile. 'I think I should go back to work.'

Mocking brows rose. 'A conscience? Or could it be because of me?'

'You?' Julie tried to make herself sound incredulous, even though panic was ready to set in. He *had* guessed. 'Why should that be?'

'Aren't you fearful that your—er—that Ian might object to you lying here with another man?'

She gave a tiny gulp. He had been going to say husband, in that derogatory tone that spelled danger. 'I'm sure he knows I'm safe with you,' she said pertly.

His lips quirked. 'Yes, of course, perfectly safe.' And then he added quietly, 'It's the others you need to watch.'

He meant Jake, of course, but she was hardly listening. She was looking instead at his mouth, wondering what it would be like to be kissed by those lips, those generously moulded, sensually passionate lips. Her toes curled at the very thought.

'It is, however,' he said, 'almost lunchtime. No sense

in starting work again yet. I don't know about you, but that swim has intensified my appetite.'

His words cut into her concentration and Julie came back to earth with a jolt—only to find that his eyes were exploring her mouth too!

## CHAPTER FOUR

JULIE swallowed hard and knew she dared not look into Cameron's eyes. What sort of appetite was he talking about, for heaven's sake? 'Lunch sounds a perfect idea,' she agreed, and jumped to her feet, her heart throbbing fit to burst.

She knew that any sort of fleeting desires Cameron had were perfectly normal in a healthy red-blooded male who hadn't been with a woman in months—years, maybe. He had advised her to be careful of the other men in his team, especially Jake, suggesting that he himself was above that sort of thing, that he had an iron will. He very clearly hadn't counted on the fact that they would be spending fairly lengthy amounts of time in close proximity, and that these things happened whether you wanted them to or not.

Or was she doing him an injustice? Had she misinterpreted that look? Had it been, perhaps, wishful thinking on her part? By this time he had risen too, and there was nothing on his face to suggest that he found her in any way remotely desirable.

She returned to her tent and pulled a baggy T-shirt over her bikini and they sat in the shade to eat the sandwiches she had prepared earlier. Cameron, to her relief, began talking about his work.

'Ecology has always been a passionate interest of mine. I was forever querying why one plant thrived in a different place from another, why this animal did this and that one something else. So much so that my parents sometimes got exasperated with me because they could never answer all of my questions.'

'I bet they're proud of you now.'

His mouth twisted and a shadow darkened his eyes. 'They're divorced.' It was said succinctly, and it was obvious it troubled him deeply. 'My father lives in New Zealand—he's married again—and my mother lives alone in London. I don't see either of them very often, unfortunately.'

'I'm sorry.'

He shook his head. 'Don't be; it happened a long time ago.'

'Was there someone else involved?' It was a highly personal question, and perhaps she ought not to have asked, but it was too much like what had happened to her own parents for her to let it pass without comment.

'Unfortunately, yes,' he admitted. 'My father used to be away on business a lot, much as I am now. My mother didn't mind at first, but his trips seemed to take longer and longer and she grew lonelier and lonelier.' His tone became bitter, and Julie could see that he did not enjoy casting his mind back into the past. 'She got herself a part-time job and her employer was a philandering widower and—well, I don't think I need go into the rest.'

She looked at him compassionately. 'That's why you've never married?'

'Not altogether, but you must agree my sort of lifestyle doesn't lend itself happily to marriage. I couldn't condemn a woman to a life of waiting and loneliness, and I couldn't give up what I do either. So——' he gave a tiny shrug of his broad shoulders '—I prefer to remain single.'

He was still wearing his black trunks, and although

Julie kept her mind on what he was saying she could not stop her eyes roving over his deeply tanned body. There was not one ounce of superfluous fat on him, he was in perfect physical shape and condition, and just looking at those powerful thighs was enough to send tremors of awareness through every vein.

She understood Cameron's sentiments entirely, but was not sure that she thought it a good thing for him never to get married. He did not strike her as the type of man who would be content to live into old age without a woman at his side. 'What's to stop you bringing a wife along with you?'

His laughter was highly sceptical, his blue eyes derisive. 'It might work in theory, but not practice. I've seen it. All too soon a woman craves a proper home, a proper base, a family. It's in her genes, Julie. You must know that. Would you stay out here permanently with Ian? Would you live in a tent indefinitely? For years, perhaps?'

'If I was interested in the same sort of thing I could see it working' she said thoughtfully, surprised how passionate he was about love and marriage.

Again he shrugged. 'There are women biologists, yes, who do come out in the field, but sooner or later they want to settle down in a happy little home with a happy little family.'

'My parents are divorced too.' The words popped out and Julie wondered why she had said them. What possible interest could it be to Cameron? Was she subconsciously hoping that it could form some sort of bond between them? Something to draw them closer together?

His eyes narrowed and he looked at her thoughtfully.

'It happens all too often, doesn't it, Julie? What happened in their case?'

It suddenly occurred to her that Ian could have already told him, that he could actually be testing her. She really ought to learn to keep her mouth shut. 'The usual,' she said, lifting her shoulders and trying to sound nonchalant. 'Another woman involved.'

'How old were you?'

No getting out of it now. 'Eleven,' she told him, and to her relief there was no sign on his face that he had heard the story before.

'Too young,' he agreed. 'You need a sound home-life at that age. Are you an only child?'

Julie's muscles tensed. 'No, I have a brother.'

'A brother?' he remarked thoughtfully. 'Is he older or younger?'

'Older.' At least that was the truth—even though by only half an hour—and she was able to say it with conviction.

He smiled, almost as though he could read her thoughts. 'I imagine it brought you closer together?' And the white of his teeth glinted in a very predatory way.

She swallowed hard. 'Yes.'

'*Very* close, in fact?' There was a sudden questioning lift to his brow. 'So close that you're virtually inseparable?' He moved closer towards her. 'So close that you go everywhere together, do everything together? As close as husband and wife, in fact?'

Please God, he was only guessing. Her fingers went automatically to the wedding-ring. 'We were always close,' she said huskily, 'and I think it's time I went back to work.'

She sprang to her feet and rushed over to her tent to

change back into the top and skirt she had worn earlier, but once inside she took her time, needing to calm her ragged breathing and restore her mind to some sort of order. This was awful, far worse than she had ever imagined. Cameron must know—why else would he say such things? And yet, because of Ian, she had to keep her silence; she had to carry on the pretence.

It was a vain hope that he wouldn't join her again and Julie found it impossible to concentrate. Trying to type with this highly physical man sitting less than six feet away was sheer hell. Each hour dragged interminably and it was a relief when Raul came to begin preparations for the evening meal.

She began to tidy her desk.

'What are you doing?' asked Cameron sharply.

She looked at him in surprise. 'I'm going to help Raul, of course.'

He shook his head. 'That won't be necessary; I've changed my mind.'

'What do you mean?' she asked, frowning now.

'It has occurred to me,' he said, 'that if you do the cooking as well it will hold things up here. I had not realised how much typing there was. I want it brought up to date quickly, so that once we're on Vulcan you can give my book your full attention. Raul can stay on.'

'But don't you think Raul might have plans of his own?' she asked. Did he always ride roughshod over people's arrangements? Did he always think that he only had to click his fingers to get what he wanted?

Cameron shook his head decisively. 'I doubt it. Raul's never been anywhere in his life. He's never left these islands. He was grateful for the job. It was my suggestion he had some time off. I'm sure he won't mind.' He made it sound as though he was doing Raul a favour. 'You look disappointed. I thought you didn't fancy cooking for the multitudes, as you so drolly put it.'

'It will make a change,' she said. 'It will give me a break.' And it would take her out of the tent at this particular moment, give her breathing space. She had been closeted with him for almost the whole day and it was beginning to tell on her nerves.

'My mind is made up,' he announced firmly. 'I need you here more. Have you any idea how long all this will take?' There was a different atmosphere between them now. Since that heartstopping moment on the beach he had given no indication of being attracted to her. Maybe she *had* imagined it.

'I would say just a couple of days if I have no interruptions,' she answered. And if she could stand the pace in this heat! Already her neck was aching again, though this time she had no intention of letting Cameron know. His touch would be more than she could stand; she would be in very grave danger of giving herself away.

'That is good,' he said, 'because I am anxious to get to Vulcan as soon as possible.'

Julie, personally, was not looking forward to it. There would be no escape—from Cameron, from her thoughts, from her emotions, from anything. And on top of that would be the increasing pressure of trying to keep up appearances. And how they were going to do that when he was even now highly suspicious, she did not know. Ian would feel it too, she felt sure. She heaved a sigh. Two days and one night she had been here, and already the implications of their deception were tremendous.

She related some of her fears to Ian later. The whole evening had been fraught with tension as far as Julie was concerned, especially when Jake had tried to monopolise her again, and she had escaped early, but she was still not asleep when her twin turned in.

Sitting up in bed, with her hands clutched about her knees, she said, 'I'm scared, Ian; I'm convinced Cameron knows. He keeps making subtle hints about our relationship.'

Ian shook his head dismissively. 'You're imagining it. He's never said anything to me.'

'I'm not,' she insisted. 'He's just waiting for us to slip up, I know he is. I wish you wouldn't keep your head in the sand. Haven't you noticed anything at all?'

'Nothing,' he answered. 'He's always more than friendly.' And no matter what she said he still thought there was no likelihood of Cameron discovering they were brother and sister.

To Julie's relief, Cameron spent no more time at camp, having evidently satisfied himself that she was up to the work. She took time off during the hottest part of each day, to swim and cool herself down, but it was not so much fun on her own.

On Cameron's return each evening they discussed the notes she had typed, and although Julie struggled desperately against her attraction for him, telling herself that it was a futile, senseless emotion, she could not stop herself feeling excited when they stood close. It was impossible not to breathe him in, almost to taste his essential maleness.

And once the notes were finished, once Cameron declared they were ready to leave for Vulcan, Julie's fears increased.

Ian, on the other hand, was pulsing with excitement. To work alone with the great Cameron Storm was his dearest wish, and on the morning they were to depart he was up at the crack of dawn, waking Julie too. 'Come on, come on. Get yourself ready.'

She was nowhere near as thrilled; the whole trip spelled disaster. How could they possibly keep their secret living in such close proximity? Cameron would be sure to tell that they weren't lovers now.

After breakfast the three of them, plus Jake—who was going to bring the boat back for use by other team members in their absence—took the Jeep to the harbour where the cabin cruiser was anchored. Everything they would need had already been loaded.

Climbing on board *Sea Lady*, Julie somehow caught her toe and stumbled, and when Cameron held out his hand to steady her the current of electricity that shot through her body was tangible evidence of the trials that were to come.

Quickly she snatched away, missing his sharp frown, and ducked into the cabin, intending to remain there until her cheeks had cooled and she felt able to face him without giving away her inner torment. She really had tried to be strong where Cameron was concerned, but it wasn't working very well.

She stood staring out of the window, watching Santa Cruz get smaller and smaller, wishing she weren't quite so responsive to Cameron. If she wasn't careful it would be her downfall.

Suddenly his voice came from behind her, and as she had not heard him enter the cabin, had not sensed his presence, she gave a startled jump, turning around to face him with saucer-like eyes, her heart pitter-pattering within her breast.

'What are you doing?' he asked roughly. He wore blue denims today and a T-shirt, and he looked devastatingly masculine.

Julie lifted her shoulders and tried to sound casual. 'Just looking, just watching.' His nearness caused a stampede, pulses racing desperately out of time with each other.

'You could do that on deck.'

'I'll come up in a minute,' she said quietly, trying to make it sound as though nothing was wrong.

But he did not leave it there. His blue eyes pierced hers, as if trying to look into the very depths of her mind. 'What is wrong, Julie?'

Her heart hammered, but she shook her head and tried to deny her fears. 'Nothing.'

Cameron's eyes narrowed disbelievingly. 'Nothing, and you're behaving like this? I believe you're lying. I believe we have a very considerable problem—don't think I didn't notice that you snatched away from me like a scalded cat.' His lips tightened as he spoke. 'But—as we're to work and live so closely together—I suggest you hide your dislike of me, or whatever it is that is festering in your mind, otherwise this whole undertaking will be a disaster. Is that understood?'

It was a relief that he had misread her action, a welcome relief. Julie felt herself smiling. Life would be a whole lot easier if he really thought that she did not like him. 'I'll try,' she said.

'You'll do more than try,' he barked, 'otherwise you and Ian will be back in England before you know what's hit you. We work as a team here or not at all.' His harsh tone scraped over her nerve-endings like a piece of coarse sandpaper. 'Now, I suggest you get back on deck and start behaving yourself.' He stood back for her to precede him.

Jake was steering and he smiled at her cheerfully, seeming to see nothing wrong. 'This is the life, eh?'

She paused at his side. 'It's lovely, isn't it? How we long for perfect blue skies such as this in England.'

He grinned. 'A typical Pommy, always talking about the weather.'

Julie laughed. 'I guess we do; we're never satisfied.'

'I suppose you'll be complaining of the heat next?' he jeered good-humouredly.

'I'm already finding it a trifle enervating,' she agreed, still smiling.

'You'll get used to it.' And then, in a much lower, conspiratorial tone, 'It's a pity you and Ian couldn't be alone. Castaways on a desert island and all that. The boss will be a real thorn in your side.'

Julie looked cautiously at Cameron, who was now talking to Ian, and answered in an equally low voice, 'Don't you believe it.'

Jake evidently thought she and Ian had already made their plans and he roared with knowing laughter, causing the others to look at them with sudden questioning interest. Ian merely smiled when he caught her eye, but Cameron frowned harshly, and when a few minutes later she left Jake's side to join her brother, who was now sitting on the foredeck, he waylaid her.

'It's a dangerous game you're playing, *Mrs* Drummond.' His blue eyes were hidden behind a pair of dark sunglasses, but his lean body was tense.

'What do you mean?'

'You and Jake.'

She gave a laugh. 'Jake is merely being friendly.'

'Too friendly,' he growled.

'You're seeing things that are not there,' she said tightly.

'Am I?' Brows slid smoothly upwards. 'You've made your preferences very clear, but it's Ian I feel sorry for.'

Julie's eyes flashed. 'Ian knows there's nothing between Jake and me, and if he doesn't object to me talking to him then I don't see why you should.'

'So long as *talking* is all you do,' he warned. 'From my point of view I think you should pay more attention to your *husband*. You spend remarkably little time together—considering.'

Be careful, Julie, be careful, she warned herself, don't say something you'll regret. 'It's difficult,' she said quietly, 'when he's so busy all the time.'

'Is that a complaint?' Blue eyes glittered dangerously and menacingly.

'Of course not,' she answered. Why did he insist on misinterpreting everything she said? 'I understood the position before I came. You're making mountains out of molehills, Mr Storm. Ian isn't complaining about the situation, and nor am I.'

He looked at her closely, intently, and Julie knew it was imperative that she change the subject. She gave a wide, hopefully reassuring smile. 'I like the boat. It's very nice.'

'It does the job,' he growled.

'Do you ever sleep on it?' She had noticed two berths.

'Rarely.' He seemed impatient with her questioning, as though he knew it was a ploy on her part. 'It's used mainly to ferry the team around. Do you like boats?'

'I've never really been on one,' she admitted.

Eyebrows rose. 'Now that is strange——' and his eyes

looked deeply into hers '—because Ian definitely told me that you spent your honeymoon cruising the Greek Islands.'

Julie gave an embarrassed laugh that was half a cough. 'A cruise liner hardly counts, does it? It's more like a hotel.' Damn! What else had he told this man, for heaven's sake? How careful did she have to be? Lord, the whole thing was like treading on eggshells.

'You mean,' he challenged mockingly, 'that you were so taken up with each other that you hardly noticed your surroundings?'

Julie hated his taunts, and it took all her willpower not to retaliate. 'Something like that.'

'I guess the honeymoon stage finished quickly.' An eyebrow quirked. 'I haven't noticed any urgency on either part to fall into each other's arms. Maybe you should join your—husband now?' he suggested with a wicked smile. 'And make the most of the next hour or so. Once we're on Vulcan he'll be working so hard that you definitely won't see much of him.'

Julie gladly took the excuse to escape, joining her brother on the foredeck, sitting down beside him and heaving a troubled sigh.

'What's wrong, Sis?'

Why was he so singularly blind? she wondered. 'This,' she hissed. 'Cameron, you and me—everything.'

He looked at her with a questioning frown.

'He just mentioned our "honeymoon". We were talking about boats. I almost put my foot in it. I didn't know you'd told him we'd been cruising. What else is there I should know?'

Ian put his big capable hand over hers. 'Lord, I don't know; we've talked about all sorts of things. Don't worry so much; I have complete faith in you. You're good at improvising. I know you won't let me down.'

'Not deliberately,' she whispered fiercely, 'but it's all getting a bit too much. I don't know whether I can cope.'

'Will you quit looking so enraged?' he admonished. 'Or Cameron really will think there's something wrong.' He draped his arm about her and Julie dropped her head on his shoulder.

'I'm sorry,' she said, managing a wan smile, 'but he's even accused me of making a play for Jake. The man's unbelievable.'

'That, I can understand,' said Ian, 'though I think it's the other way round. Jake seems very taken with you.'

Julie looked horrified. 'Surely not? You're wrong; he's just being friendly.'

'That's not what it looks like,' he warned her. 'And I'm not the only one who thinks so.'

'So oughtn't you to be playing the irate husband?' she asked. 'Lord, Ian, the success of our plan depends as much on you as me.'

'Take it easy, Sis.' He grinned. 'Once we're on Vulcan nothing can go wrong.'

'Cameron thinks you're not loving enough.'

'Then I'll be loving. I don't want to ruin everything at this stage. Working alone with Cameron is far more than I'd ever imagined. It's such an honour. I'm so proud and so happy.' His arm tightened about her shoulders, but Julie was all too conscious of Cameron's piercing eyes on their backs.

However, when a school of dolphins playfully rushed along in their bow-wave, calling out to each other in happy, high-pitched squeaks, she became totally entranced and was able to forget her uneasiness for a while.

Vulcan was one of the most westerly islands in the archipelago and it seemed remarkably small as they approached, with steep rocky sides that made landing look impossible. 'Is this it?' she enquired incredulously.

'This is it,' Cameron agreed. He had taken over from Jake and was steering the boat skilfully. Julie could still not see anywhere to land and was amazed when a tiny inlet emerged between the volcanic cliffs and a long, narrow, dazzling coral beach became visible.

He dropped anchor and they made several journeys with the dinghy to take their supplies ashore. Unable to stand back and let the men do all the work, Julie helped load the numerous boxes and bags, even a small Calor-gas refrigerator! It was surprising how much they needed.

She and Jake were laughing over one particularly heavy crate, that between them they were trying to heave into position ready for handing down into the dinghy, when Cameron barked loudly, 'Enough! Julie, leave it. Jake, you steady the dinghy.'

His brow was as black as a storm-cloud and Julie felt a quiver of fear; she had not even realised he'd returned from his last trip. Even Jake looked suprised at the harshness of his tone.

With remarkable alacrity Jake jumped into the dinghy while Cameron climbed back on board and tied a rope around the crate, before lowering it down and then making a signal for Jake to take the tiny boat ashore.

Julie felt impending disaster.

'Didn't my warning make any difference?' he barked.

'I was merely helping Jake.'

Dark brows rose. 'It didn't look like that to me. I was afraid something like this would happen the moment I set eyes on you.'

'And what is that supposed to mean?' she riposted. She was finding it very difficult to understand him. He had given her a lecture on hiding her dislike and yet he was making his very clear. It was definitely a no-win situation, a one-sided affair.

'You respond to flattery like flower petals to the sun, that's what it means,' he growled.

Julie shook her head. 'This is unbelievable. Go ask Ian what I'm like, he'll soon tell you that you're making a mistake. I'm not interested in Jake.'

Cameron gave a twisted smile. 'I've no doubt Ian knows *very* well indeed what you're like.'

Julie let out an exasperated sigh. 'So you're going to stick to your opinion that I flirt with every single man I meet? What's going to happen when the three of us are alone on Vulcan? Will you accuse me of making a play for you then?'

He gave a loud guffaw. 'I don't think you'd dare, which is a blessing, because having to continually reject your advances would certainly make the next few weeks very difficult.'

'You swine!' Julie lifted her hand to strike him, but again thought better of it and turned away. Almost immediately, however, she swung back to face him. 'You're a bastard, do you know that? Getting a job with you was the worst thing Ian ever did.'

'And I'm beginning to think it was the worst thing I ever did suggesting he bring his wife with him,' Cameron returned brutally. 'I thought I was doing him a favour. Instead it would appear I've done myself a great disservice.'

# CHAPTER FIVE

JULIE'S eyes flashed into Cameron's face. 'I beg your pardon? You were doing Ian no favour. All you were after was a copy-typist and a cook—free, gratis and for nothing. I don't believe you would have made such a suggestion if I hadn't had the necessary qualifications. No other men have brought their wives, and I know some of them are married because Jake told me.'

'Jake told you?' Disapproving brows rose yet again. 'You would appear to have had some deep and meaningful discussions.'

'And you have a sick mind,' she retorted. 'But you can think what you like; my conscience is clear.' Out of the corner of her eye she could see Jake coming back with the dinghy, and knew he must be wondering what was going on. He had no idea that Cameron had warned her off him, that his chief saw things that were not there. She moved to the other side of the cruiser, watching the mocking-birds and the boobies who were showing a keen interest in all the activity.

'That's the lot,' Cameron announced brusquely as Jake climbed on board. 'You can take *Sea Lady* back now. I'll see you in a month's time. You've got the list of food we'll need?'

Jake nodded.

He was bringing *more* supplies! 'How long are we going to stay?' she asked, panic in her voice.

'As long as it takes,' came Cameron's curt response, which was no answer at all as far as she was concerned.

Jake lifted an eyebrow as he looked at Julie, telling her without words that he did not understand what was going on, but that she had his sympathies.

'Goodbye, Jake,' she said, as she began to climb down into the bobbing dinghy, 'I'll see you in a month, I guess.'

Cameron followed her, started the outboard motor, and they skimmed the waves as they left *Sea Lady* behind and joined Julie's brother on Vulcan Island.

It did not take the men long to erect the tents and to Julie's delight and amazement she and Ian each had one of their own.

'We always use these smaller tents when we sojourn on other islands,' Cameron remarked coolly. 'I do apologise. I trust it won't put too much strain on your—*relationship*.' He looked pointedly at Julie as he spoke.

Ian answered. 'Think nothing of it—we'll survive. What do you say, Julie?' He put his arm about her and she smiled up into his face.

'I'll try not to complain.'

Cameron's eyes were unreadable behind his dark glasses, but there was an irritatingly mocking curve to his lips and Julie turned away. 'I'll get us something to eat.'

While the men were erecting their sleeping quarters she had sorted and stacked their food supplies into the store tent—and still the mocking-birds watched and waited, and Julie knew she would have to be careful that they did not steal their precious food.

Their cooking stove was nothing like as big as the one at the main camp: still fuelled by Calor gas but with only a couple of rings and a grill. They had sea bass and boiled potatoes, and fresh papaya for dessert, eating at a collapsible table they had also brought with them. It was not very big and twice Julie's knee touched Cameron's and she jerked away, and on each occasion he frowned—and she knew exactly what he was thinking.

It had taken them all day to get here and set up camp and in another hour it would be dark. Julie could not wait to go to bed. She desperately needed to put some space between her and Cameron. His attitude was getting to her like nothing else ever had. She was amazed Ian could not see it.

'I made a solar still the last time I was here,' Cameron informed Ian. 'I suggest we check and see if it's still in good condition.'

Although they had brought fresh water with them, collecting their own potable water would be a great help in supplementing supplies, Julie realised. They would still need to use sea-water and sea-soap to bathe and wash their clothes, however, and that was something she knew she would never get used to, despite her brother's reassurances.

In their absence, Julie explored the surrounding area and found a tempting tidal rock-pool not far away from their camp. Without stopping to think, she stripped off her loose cotton dress and immersed herself in the water, disturbing dozens of brightly coloured Sally Lightfoot crabs as she did so.

In parts it was quite deep, and she was pleasantly surprised to discover that it had been warmed by the heat of the day's sun. In fact it was sheer bliss, and she stayed in much longer than she'd intended, so long, in fact, that the men returned in her absence and it was not Ian who came to find her, but Cameron!

There was no escape, nowhere at all to hide, and she

looked at him in alarm, though she hid it with a smile of greeting.

'So this is where you've got to.' The dark glasses were gone and he looked thoroughly amused to have found her in such a compromising situation.

Julie's heart thudded wildly. 'I didn't realise I'd been away so long. This pool is wonderful. If you'd just, er——' she made a vague gesture with her hands for him to go away '—I'll——'

He picked up the dress she had tossed on to the black volcanic rock. 'There's no place for modesty here, Julie, and least of all coming from you.'

His dig hurt, and she could not understand it, but before she could retort he held out his hand. 'Let me help you; these rocks can be lethal.'

Against her better judgement, Julie allowed him to steady her as she climbed out, and she had almost made it when, at the last second, her foot slipped on the algae. If it had not been for Cameron's instant reaction she would have fallen backwards into the water, might even have hurt herself on the rocks.

As they both fought to maintain their balance she was pulled hard against his disturbing male body. It was for seconds only and yet the blood surged through Julie's veins, her heart pounding so hard it felt as though it was trying to escape from her ribcage.

Cameron swiftly wrapped the dress around her and set her away from him. 'I don't think it a good idea that you bathe here alone,' he said roughly. 'You see how easy it is to have an accident. I think you'd better wait for Ian to join you another time.'

She wanted to say that if he hadn't been here it wouldn't have happened, but that would perhaps give away her inner torment. It was best she remain silent.

'Some of that rock can be razor-sharp,' he added. 'I shudder to think what would have happened if I hadn't saved you.'

'I'm grateful,' she said demurely.

He looked at her with suspicion, having clearly expected a heated retort. 'I think we'd best get back,' he announced gruffly, 'or Ian will be wondering what the hell's going on.'

Julie was actually surprised that her twin hadn't come looking for her. He shouldn't give Cameron the opportunity of confirming his suspicions that their relationship wasn't all they claimed it to be. He had said he would be more loving, so why wasn't he being?

Her brother looked up from his notebook as they approached, his smile welcoming. 'So you found her.'

Cameron grunted, and Ian frowned and looked questioningly at Julie. She lifted her shoulders and pulled down the corners of her mouth. 'I've been bathing,' she said needlessly.

The sun had turned the sea to molten gold and the black volcanic rocks to bronze. Even Julie's faint sun-tan took on a healthy glow, and it would have been perfect had the situation not been so delicate.

'I was going to come looking for you myself,' Ian said, 'but Cameron quite rightly said that he knew the island better than me and that he had a good idea where you were.'

And that was supposed to make her feel better, she thought as she ducked into her tent and pulled on a pair of white cotton trousers and a pink shirt, knotting it beneath her breasts. She was still vividly aware of the fact that Cameron had seen her naked and her whole body tingled at the thought of what could have happened.

It was at times like this that she regretted their subterfuge. On the other hand, if she hadn't agreed to her brother's risky plan, she would never have met Cameron and the situation wouldn't have arisen. It was a vicious circle and there was no way out of it.

They sat long after it got dark, letting the stars and the waning moon be their canopy of light. The men spoke of all manner of things, mostly connected with the islands, and Julie listened to the cadences in Cameron's voice, the soft, deep tones when he was quietly passionate, the deeper, more resonant sounds when he was excited.

'What do you think, Julie?'

She suddenly realised that she was being spoken to and that she hadn't heard a word that was said. She had been mesmerised by his voice, not what he was saying, and now she looked at him and gave a guilty smile. 'I'm sorry, I wasn't listening.'

'We thought you might like to join us tomorrow, rather than stay here by yourself.'

Julie looked cautiously from Cameron to her brother and back again, wondering whose idea it had been. 'I don't think so. I think I should make a start on your book.'

'On the contrary.' Blue eyes pierced hers. 'I think you should familiarise yourself with the island first. It's not large, only two and a half square kilometres, but if you need us for any reason you'll want to know roughly where to find us. I shall always tell you our plans for the day.'

It sounded reasonable, but Julie glanced at her twin for approval before inclining her head. 'Whatever you say.'

Cameron gave a growl of anger, for some reason her

answer displeasing him. Perhaps she hadn't been enthusiastic enough? 'Getting the lie of the land is pure common sense, for both of you.' He got up from his chair and walked away, disappearing into the blackness of the night.

'What's got into him?' asked Ian. 'He's been like a bear with a sore head ever since we got here.'

'He's angry with me,' she told him sadly.

'Whatever for?'

'Because of Jake—again. Lord, I hate Cameron; he's impossible. I don't know how I'm going to get through the next few weeks.'

'You'll manage, Sis,' Ian assured her.

And she knew that for his sake she would do her best, but would her best be good enough?

At nine o'clock she and Ian decided to go to bed. There was nothing to do and Cameron would probably get them up early tomorrow. Sunrise was a swift quarter of an hour affair at about six, and everyone was always awake by then. She saw no reason why Cameron would do anything different here.

Julie must have been more tired than she thought, because she dropped immediately to sleep and knew nothing more until she heard Cameron bellowing at her to wake up.

She groaned and squinted at her wristwatch. True to form, six o'clock. 'I'm coming,' she called.

'Ian isn't well,' he announced, the second she showed her head outside the tent.

Immediately she was full of concern, frowning as she entered her brother's tent. 'What's wrong?' she asked worriedly as she saw his pale face.

He groaned. 'It's just a migraine, there's no panic.'

He had been getting them on and off ever since his split-up with Julie, but none since he'd been out here. She wondered what had brought this one on now. 'Where are your tablets?' she asked.

Guessing that this would put paid to their explorations, Julie was totally astonished after breakfast when Cameron announced that their plans were unchanged, the two of them were going without Ian.

'I can't leave him like this,' she protested.

'He says he would prefer to be left alone.'

Julie pulled a wry face. 'He always does, but I'm not sure that out here it's very wise.'

'I appreciate your concern,' said Cameron drily, 'but I consider today's explorations a vital and very necessary part of your education.'

Their eyes met and warred but Julie knew that she really had no choice. she was going to have to spend the whole day with Cameron whether she liked it or not.

It was with severe misgivings that Julie set off with Cameron on their tour of the island. Ian had assured her that he would be all right, that he preferred to be on his own, that he would be no company if she stayed.

'But I would be company for you,' she insisted.

'I don't want company,' he told her wearily. 'I just want to lie here until I feel better. Bring me a jug of water if you like, but that's all I need.'

And so, reluctantly, she had gone, conscious of the fact that it was going to be a very difficult day. Cameron Storm had got under her skin to such an extent that she was too aware of him for her own good. It would be hard, if not impossible, to keep her feelings hidden for much longer. The more she saw of him the worse it became to pretend he meant nothing to her. This whole exercise had been meant to rid her mind of Roger—it had done that all right, but in so doing had added another complication to her life.

Like any other island in the archipelago, Vulcan was much drier close to shore, and because it was still a relatively new island only a few parched cacti had begun to grow and the occasional tangled, thorny scrub poked out of fissures in the rock.

'It's actually much greener than usual,' Cameron told her, 'because we had rain just before you came.'

Julie believed him but it certainly didn't look like it; everywhere was wild and barren and most unwelcoming. She was not really sure that she was looking forward to spending any length of time here. She liked Santa Cruz much better. Or was it because there were other people there and she felt safer?

He showed her the solar still—a tarred wooden box about three feet by eight and six inches deep, lined with black polythene and filled with sea-water. 'Ian and I replaced the polythene yesterday,' he told her. Stretched over the box was a clear plastic roof, like a miniature greenhouse, curved under on the inside to form a trough. The whole structure was tilted slightly.

'The idea is,' explained Cameron, 'that the sun's heat is absorbed by the black polythene, thus producing vapour which condenses on the roof and runs down into the troughs. It then falls, drip by meagre drip, into these containers. Some goes back into the tank, unfortunately, but by trial and error I've managed to make the whole thing fairly efficient. We probably get about a gallon of water a day.'

'I'm impressed,' said Julie.

'It's primitive but it works,' he said, 'though I can't take credit for the original idea. But enough time spent here—let's get moving.'

She had plaited and coiled her hair high on her head, perching her straw hat on top. She wore a pair of loose cotton trousers and a T-shirt, and thick-soled trainers which gave her protection against the sometimes vicious edges of the solidified lava.

He took her hand as they scaled the cliffs above their camp. 'Do I have to climb up here if I need to come looking for you or Ian?' she asked as they paused for rest. She was slightly breathless, and hoped Cameron wouldn't guess that it was more because of his touch than the exertion.

'Is it too much for you?' Blue eyes mocked her.

'Of course not,' she said with an airy grin. 'I'm as fit as a fiddle. But it does seem a lengthy procedure. Isn't there anywhere else on the island we could camp where access is easier?'

His lips curled down expressively. 'I'm afraid not. This is one of the least accessible islands, but it has the advantage of keeping the tourists away. They're becoming a problem, I'm afraid.'

'Why is that?' she asked.

'Because,' he explained with surprising patience, 'there are plants on these islands that are unique; it would be catastrophic if they got trampled on and destroyed altogether. That's why there are visitor centres on most islands, and specific trails from which you must not wander. A guide is always necessary.'

'Is that why it's been turned into a National Park?'

'Absolutely,' he told her.

The climbing was easier now, the atmosphere more humid, and the hostile prickly pear had changed to a mixture of much kinder bushes and trees.

'I don't know whether your beloved husband has explained,' he went on, 'but all of these islands are the tips of volcanoes, pushed up through the ocean when eruptions took place. These on the western side are the most newly formed and are still active.'

Ian hadn't told her, and she looked at him now, wide-eyed. 'Active? Is it safe?'

Cameron laughed. 'Let's say I wouldn't be here if I didn't think so. Scientists these days constantly monitor the amount of activity in volcanoes.'

'I hope you're right,' she murmured.

The ground levelled out a bit and Julie made sure there was more space between her and Cameron. It had become virtually impossible to breathe without drinking him in. They were faced with what looked like a field of black lava, which had cooled into fantastic shapes. Here and there mosses and ferns had started to grow and Julie was completely mesmerised by it.

'It's beautiful.' Her voice was hushed, almost as though it were a sacred place.

Cameron made no comment and she turned to look at him; he was watching her, closely observing the light and excitement and appreciation in her eyes.

Julie's breath caught in her throat and a tremor ran through her—her own tiny eruption! His expression was like none she had seen before. For that tiny space of time he was completely caught up in her. Their eyes met and locked and he, too, seemed to have difficulty tearing away.

The spell was broken when he spoke and it was like the fracturing of an exquisite piece of crystal, the whole moment shattered in a brilliant display of reflected sunlight. Julie could almost see the dazzling colours and she had no idea what he'd said.

'I'm sorry,' she whispered through parched lips, 'I didn't hear you.'

He gave a twisted smile. 'I said, it is unusual to find a kindred spirit.'

'What do you mean?' Had he guessed how she felt? Still her breathing was erratic, her mouth so dry that swallowing became difficult. It was such a dangerous situation; she must not, could not get tangled with this man, not if she wanted to safeguard her brother's job.

'To some people this volcanic landscape means nothing,' he said. 'In fact they find it quite ugly.'

She smiled in relief. 'I see.' She had been worrying for nothing. It was the beauty of the scene he wanted to discuss, not themselves, not her feelings.

'"I see"?' he repeated quizzically. 'Is that all you have to say?'

Her hands fluttered in a gesture of helplessness. 'No, of course not. I—I wasn't aware that you knew how I felt.'

'You have an expressive face, Julie. There is nothing you can hide from me.'

A wave of trepidation washed over her, but she was grateful for the warning, and made a vow to be extra careful in future. 'This scenery is certainly impressive,' she said. 'I can't quite get over all the shapes and forms. Some of them look like faces, some like coiled ropes. It's fascinating.'

She skipped on ahead of him, looking intently at the lavascape, giving it her full attention so that she would not have to face Cameron and the chaotic emotions churning inside her.

'Isn't it?' He had moved silently closer, his voice disturbing in her ear, the electric vibes of him shooting across the short distance between them.

Julie knew that to move would give the game away, disclose to Cameron exactly how she felt, even though he might mistakenly think it was hatred. But to stay put was equally as dangerous. Surely he could hear the unsteady beat of her heart? Feel the heat of her skin, which had nothing to do with the hot sun pouring down on them? She was glad she had worn her hat; she tugged at the brim now, hiding her eyes beneath it.

'Each island is unique in its own right,' he told her. 'No two are the same. There are different forms of lava as well, though I won't bore you with detail. Let us climb a little higher so that we can observe the whole island. I can then point out the sites where Ian and myself are likely to work.'

It was a release to get going again, though he didn't move far from her side, and once or twice he held out his hand to steady her as they climbed over uneven ground. She was careful not to snatch away.

The day was turning out to be far worse than Julie had anticipated. It was impossible to ignore the galaxy of feelings and sensations that insisted on twisting her stomach into knots and running riot through her bloodstream.

At the top they looked down into the collapsed crater and also out across the island. The views were stunning. Not only could they see the whole of Vulcan, but all of the other islands as well, looking like giant cinders dropped into the Pacific Ocean from a great height.

'I'm moved,' she said. 'It's like being in another world.'

He looked pleased. 'When I suggested Ian bring his—wife——' a slight pause, but it could have been her imagination '—I did not expect someone who would enthuse over these islands as I do. Most people, and I'm not talking about scientists now, find them fascinating as far as the wildlife is concerned, because it's different and varied and unusual, but as for the islands themselves——' he lifted his shoulders in an expressive shrug '—they're not their usual concept of an island in the Pacific.'

'They expect something like Hawaii or Tahiti?' she asked with a laugh. 'I agree, but it's because they're different that I like them. I think the lava is beautiful—in its own way.'

Julie suddenly realised that by enthusing like this she was in danger of drawing herself and Cameron too close together—and this was what she could not afford to do. She turned away, looking in a different direction, exclaiming in delight when a blue-footed boobie landed almost at her feet.

They were distinctive birds, looking for all the world as though they had stepped up to their thighs into a pot of blue paint, and so tame. Ian had said they were actually called boobies because of their tameness. At least it was a distraction, and she concentrated all her attention on it.

'I think we should move on.' Cameron's voice sounded much harsher all of a sudden. He hitched the backpack which contained their lunch into a more comfortable position and strode away.

Julie wondered what was wrong. It was as though some shadow had crossed their path, as though his thoughts all of a sudden had gone from her to something unpleasant. Whatever, it was perhaps for the best. There had been a very definite danger of them becoming too familiar.

From the top of the island they tramped down the other side, Cameron leading her to a shore which was not a shore really, just a rocky incline leading right down to the sea. And on this occasion he made no attempt to help her.

Julie wondered if she was the cause of his anger and tried to recall whether she had said or done anything adverse. Nothing came to mind—except that she had turned away and tried to ignore him. Was that it? Was that what was wrong? Or had he guessed how she felt about him and this was his way of dealing with it? The thought made her go hot and cold.

She had no time to dwell on these disquieting thoughts, however, because it was here that they found the fur seals—a whole colony of them. With their squat, bear-like faces and upturned noses they were entrancing.

'They're smaller than sea-lions, and less friendly,' Cameron told her. 'Probably because of the way they were once hunted. Most animals here have no fear of man at all, which is the attraction for the visitors.'

They sat on the rocks at the water's edge, Cameron dousing them liberally with water first to cool them down. The hottest part of the day was two o'clock, and as it was nearing that now it was almost impossible to walk without the heat burning through the soles of their shoes. But there was no shelter and the heat did not seem to bother Cameron.

They ate their sandwiches and drank luke-warm orange juice; unhurried, patient, silently watching the adorable creatures' antics. Cameron's mood seemed to have passed—or had he mellowed because of the seals and not her? This was his real interest, after all; humans came a poor second.

Nevertheless, Julie felt happy sitting there, enjoying his company, enjoying the feel of this exciting male animal, conscious of excitement tingling through her veins. Although her eyes were on the fur seals it was Cameron who was in her thoughts. Every second of the time they spent together she was alive to him.

When one particularly inquisitive pup came right up to Julie, its flippers on the rock at her side, its large brown eyes gazing curiously into hers, Cameron said, 'You're honoured; he must have good taste. It took me weeks the last time I was here to get them used to me.'

Julie looked at him, her heart suddenly pitter-pattering within her breast. He was watching her again, though this time there were no emotions on his face.

'How did you and Ian meet?'

It was the sixty-four thousand dollar question that she had been dreading. She had no idea whether Ian had already mentioned the real circumstances of he and the other Julie meeting. She knew what they were, but not in any detail. It was a trick question, she felt sure, asked only because Cameron was already highly suspicious.

## CHAPTER SIX

IT WENT against every principle Julie held, pretending
to be her brother's wife, and if she hadn't loved Ian so
dearly, if she hadn't wanted his happiness so very much
after the break-up of his marriage, she would never
have agreed to the deception.

'We've actually known each other all our lives,' she
told Cameron now, feeling distinctly apprehensive and
hoping it did not show in her face.

Cameron's brows rose. 'I understood it was a very
*sudden* affair?'

'Well——' Julie pulled a wry face, lifting her
shoulders in an airy gesture '—it was.' And that was no
lie, because Ian asking her to pretend to be his wife
had been sudden.

He looked amused by her unease, his eyes glinting,
his mouth quirking. 'You're saying that although you
knew each other quite well the discovery that you were
*in love* came right out of the blue?'

Again she shrugged, trying desperately to appear
nonchalant. 'Actually, I've always loved Ian.'

Blue eyes widened again. 'And he didn't *know*?'

He was making her sound stupid, and Julie knew
that if she wasn't careful honesty was going to be her
downfall. Trying to get around the truth without telling
any lies was proving to be very difficult.

The fur seal had gone away, playing at the water's
edge with his family, and Cameron was sitting much
closer to her than she would have liked. He was

wearing a pair of denim shorts and his powerfully muscled legs with their scattering of dark hairs drew her eyes like a magnet. There were just inches between them and she could smell the intoxicating maleness of him.

'Yes, he knew,' she admitted, 'but——'

'Perhaps he wasn't ready to commit himself?'

'Something like that, I guess,' she answered, smiling at last, relieved that he had put his own interpretation on the situation.

His eyes gleamed. 'Or perhaps he wasn't sure that marriage between the two of you was—exactly right? Perhaps he felt that your love for each other was— what shall I say?—familial? More like the love for a— a brother and sister, perhaps?'

Her heart went thud. His questioning confirmed without any shadow of doubt that he knew they were playing a game, or at least he was ninety-nine per cent sure. And he was trying to pressure her into admitting the truth. If only she could! But for Ian's sake she had to go on with it.

Her chin came up. 'I suppose it was like that—in the early days—but not any longer. Just because we're not in each other's arms all of the time, just because we don't spend every minute we have together making love, it doesn't mean that we're not *in* love.' Fear made her voice sharp—too sharp, perhaps.

This cat-and-mouse game was getting to her. She had to keep silent. Because if he ever found out for sure he would banish them. He was smiling now, relaxed and thoroughly enjoying himself, but no sooner the truth was out than his attitude would change; she knew that instinctively. He would have no compunction about sending them both back to England.

'Have you never had any other boyfriends?' he asked next, smoothly and with just the right amount of interest in his voice, but he did not fool her.

'There have been others,' she admitted.

'But none of them came up to Ian's standard, is that what you're saying? What did he think when you went out with someone else? Or didn't you tell him? Did you two-time him, in fact?'

'No, I did not,' she exclaimed vehemently. 'We were always free agents.'

An eyebrow rose. 'Ian sounds very accommodating. Were there recent boyfriends, just before your—er— sudden marriage, or were they all in the far distant past?'

It was all getting too much for Julie and she glared defiantly. 'I don't think that my private life has anything to do with you.'

'But I'm interested.' He pushed his face closer to hers, white teeth gleaming in a wicked smile. 'You're an intriguing woman, Julie Drummond, not at all what I expected. I want to know all about you—what makes you tick, everything.'

'And if I don't want to tell you?' she snapped, wondering if he had spotted the rapid fluttering of her pulses.

He lifted his shoulders in a slow, expansive gesture. 'Then I will be forced to think that you have something to hide.'

Julie gave a silent groan and wished desperately there was some escape. She was at his mercy as completely as a fly in a spider's web. 'There was someone,' she admitted finally, 'but. . .' Her voice tailed away; she could not go on.

'But Ian was your first and last love, is that it? What

made him finally pop the question? What was the decisive factor?' His eyes were ever watchful on her face.

Julie twisted the ring on her finger, unaware that she was doing so, racking her brains for some convincing answer that was not too far off the truth. 'I—I don't really know. It just happened. Ian——'

'It just happened?' he repeated derisively.

'Yes,' she whispered.

'Ian said, "Let's get married" and you agreed, just like that?'

Julie nodded.

'How amazing. Have you ever regretted it?'

Julie could take no more. She sprang to her feet, startling the seal pups playing close by. 'I think that's enough of this conversation. I'm hot; let's move before I bake to death.'

He controlled a knowing smile and hitched the backpack over his shoulder, and for the next hour or so they walked in relative silence, Cameron identifying various birds and animals, but asking no more uncomfortable questions.

Julie felt sure she had confirmed his suspicions and she wished for the millionth time that she had never let Ian persuade her to carry out such a dangerous deception.

When they got back Ian was much better, his migraine had virtually gone and he was in the process of cooking a meal for them. 'Have you enjoyed your day?' he asked, giving her a hug and a kiss.

Julie knew it was intended for Cameron's benefit, but it was a bit too enthusiastic, and unfortunately a bit too late to do any good now. Ian should have played the part better in the beginning.

'I saw lots of wildlife,' she said, 'all sorts, too many to mention, and the most beautiful fur seals. They're captivating animals. I can understand Cameron wanting to write about them.'

'But how did you get on with Cameron himself?' he asked quietly. Julie grinned and flashed her eyes. 'I'd rather not talk about it.'

Ian groaned. 'You've not been at each other's throats again?'

'He just asks too many questions,' she whispered fiercely. 'It's telling on my nerves, Ian. I don't know how long I can keep this up.'

'Oh, Sis.' He hugged her yet again. 'Please don't say that. Don't do it to me. I actually feel I'm beginning to live again. I'm not thinking so much about Julie, and I really do feel much better.'

She smiled wistfully. 'I'll try, you know that. Your happiness means a lot to me.'

'And yours to me,' he said. 'You're not truly unhappy, are you?'

'No, I'm not unhappy, I'm just worried—scared to death, in fact.' She linked her hands around his waist and looked up into his face. 'I love the place, I just hate the pretence.' And her tremendous attraction for Cameron was the worst problem of all.

Cameron emerged from his tent while they were still holding each other, black swimming trunks having replaced his shorts and shirt.

The good thing about her close kinship with her twin was that there was nothing forced, they genuinely enjoyed each other's company. There had been occasions in their past, before Ian was married, when if they'd had nothing else to do they had gone out together, maybe for a meal or to a disco, and anyone who did not know had always taken them for a couple. Theirs was something more than an ordinary brother-sister relationship, a bonding from birth that had never gone away. Surely enough to add credence to their lie?

But Cameron didn't seem impressed; indeed, there was a derogatory lift to his brows, and when Julie dived into her tent his mocking voice followed. 'Won't you join me for a swim, Julie? That's if Ian doesn't mind?'

'Not in the least,' her brother called out.

Julie cursed silently. She wished that for once Ian would object, anything to help support their story. She knew he was desperate to please his boss, but surely something like this went beyond the bounds of duty. He wasn't helping her at all.

She did desperately need a swim, more than anything after their marathon trek, but she wanted to get away from Cameron, not rejoin him. Now she had no choice.

Instead of her bikini she pulled on a one-piece swimsuit in black and cerise. At least she had her own tent, she thought thankfully; it hadn't been a problem sharing with Ian—he had always let her go to bed first, and he was always up and dressed and out before she woke up—but this was so much better. It gave her breathing space and it was what she needed right now.

When she emerged Cameron was already cleaving the ocean with his powerful arms. Actually, she would have preferred to use the pool she had found yesterday, but that would make it look as though she was deliberately avoiding him, so, taking a deep, fortifying breath, she ran lightly across the hot crunchy shore and joined him.

To her surprise she found that the waters in this tiny, secluded bay were not so cold as on Santa Cruz. She decided it was because of the natural rocky spur that protected it from the wide ocean, and which had hidden it from view when they arrived.

'Don't go out any further than the rocks,' Cameron warned her. 'There are extremely strong currents around these islands.'

They dived like seals and swam underwater for as long as they could hold their breath, and the brilliantly coloured fish which accompanied them were a constant source of pleasure. Julie felt her tension easing. When Cameron wasn't accusing he was excellent company.

'This is good,' she said, smiling with genuine enjoyment. 'How about we have a race to those rocks and back?'

He grinned. 'You're on.'

Julie knew she would not win—Cameron was a tremendous swimmer—but it was fun trying, and she was only a few yards behind him at the end.

'I'm impressed,' he said. 'You're an excellent swimmer for a girl, and much better company when you're not hating me quite so much.'

His compliment took her by surprise. 'Put my irritability down to the heat,' she said lightly. 'It's not really anything personal.'

An eyebrow rose. 'If that is the case then I've found the perfect answer to your bad moods.'

Julie gave a faint, quizzical frown.

'I shall just pick you up and dump you in the ocean.'

'You wouldn't dare!' she cried, laughing.

'Wouldn't I?' he asked warningly. 'Don't ever challenge me, Julie. I'm not one to back down.'

When they waded back to shore Julie felt happier than she had all day. They actually seemed to be achieving some kind of rapport; she flashed him a happy smile and then cried out in agony as a sharp pain pierced her foot.

She was immediately swung up into Cameron's strong arms, held against his hard, masculine body, and for an insane moment the pain was forgotten. All she could feel was the heat and the power of him.

'A sting-ray,' he declared grimly as he examined Julie's foot a few seconds later, her brother looking on anxiously. 'They do bask in the shallows on certain beaches but I've never come across any here. I'm afraid it's going to be very sore and painful for a day or two.'

It was almost worth the pain, thought Julie, to be treated with such concern, to have Cameron's undivided attention. It didn't even hurt while he was tending the wound; she was conscious only of his nearness and the effect he was having on her.

Not until she was in bed did she begin to feel the sting. Her whole leg throbbed and it kept her awake, and she wanted more than anything to have Cameron at her side.

Through the opening in her tent she watched the dawn, a glorious spectrum of colours that constantly changed the sky and the water through greys and purples and reds to gold. She listened to the by now familiar sound of the mocking-birds, scavenging for leftover pieces of food, the scratching of a finch on her tent roof, and then, through her limited field of vision, she saw Cameron walk down to the water's edge.

The tide was in, and much closer to their tents than when they had pitched them. Julie's heart began its familiar drumming, almost painful in its intensity. He wore white swimming trunks this morning and they complemented and emphasised his tan; his body was magnificent.

He walked with the grace of a feral animal and Julie looked after him hungrily. He carried his snorkel and mask and a container of some sort, and as he entered the water he shuffled his feet. She imagined it was in case there were any more sting-rays lurking. Already Julie had made up her mind that she would restrict her bathing to the lagoon.

He headed towards the outcrop of rocks, disappearing beneath the water for a considerable length of time, although if she looked really hard she could occasionally see the tip of his snorkel.

When he finally emerged it looked as though he had something in the basket, though she could not make out what it was. She called his name and he came to her tent, holding his prize out for her to see. 'Our supper,' he told her.

Julie's mouth twisted in dismay when she saw three lobsters. 'You're not expecting me to cook them?'

'It is your job,' he announced severely, and then he smiled. 'But I'll let you off since you have a bad foot. How is it this morning?' His wet hair clung to his well-shaped head, dripping down his face and off his chin, his whole body glistening, the sun behind him emphasising his breadth and strength.

Julie drew in a ragged breath. How could he affect her like this so soon after Roger? After she had sworn never to let herself get interested in any man again? It was an ironic twist of fate.

'Still painful; I've hardly slept,' she admitted. 'But I'm going to get up now and take a swim in the lagoon.'

'I'll join you,' he said at once.

'That's not necessary.'

Brows rose warningly. 'I happen to think it is.'

Julie wished Ian was awake so that she could suggest he go with her, but there was no movement at all from his tent. She shrugged. 'If you insist.' Though she could not quite see the point in it. It was only a stone's throw away. She could yell if anything happened.

He disappeared with the lobsters and she pulled on her swimsuit, but by the time she emerged from her tent he was back again, supporting her when she found it too painful to put her foot to the ground.

Again, physical contact counteracted the soreness of her wound. She felt as though she could have walked a hundred miles with him at her side, and she could not help but fantasise about what it would have been like if there was only her and Cameron here! No lies to form a barrier between them, just overwhelming joy that they were together.

She discovered the lobsters in a tiny pool next to the one where they were to swim. 'It makes a superb holding tank,' he told her.

'I'm glad you didn't put them in here.' She grinned as she slid into the water. Although they did have the company of a few small orange-bellied fish, which had been washed in through cracks in the rocks.

With high tide the lagoon was much deeper than the day before, and the water had been chilled by the cooler night air. It was certainly not so tempting to stay in for very long; just enough to revitalise and refresh—and be too aware of her companion for her own good!

Her foot did not hurt while she was swimming. It was not until she got out of the crystal-clear water and put her foot to the ground without thinking that her limitations made themselves felt.

Cameron's arm was immediately beneath hers; in

fact he hardly left her side. Although she hadn't needed him while swimming, he seemed to have made it his duty to look after her.

He helped her to level ground, and quite how it happened Julie did not know, but one second they were laughing, and the next their smiles had faded and he had pulled her against him with a groan, his mouth capturing hers in a kiss that was filled with animal hunger.

Violent shock waves ran through each and every one of Julie's veins, her nerve-endings tingling with excitement. There was no time to stop and think that it was wrong and highly dangerous, that she oughtn't to be letting him do this. This was here and now, an instant thing that neither of them could stop.

His mouth ravaged hers, and to her horror she found herself responding, straining her pulsing body against him, unable to contain the depth of passion that shuddered through every inch of her. And although the kiss lasted for seconds only, her breathing grew as deep and erratic as if she had run around the island.

When he thrust her from him, when his eyes blazed fiercely into hers, she thought for a minute that he was going to accuse her of instigating the kiss. He seemed to be struggling to find the right words, and she was ready with her answer—until he swung abruptly away and marched back to their camp, leaving her to limp along as best she could.

In one respect Julie blamed herself. She ought to have stopped him; she ought never to have allowed the kiss, not even let their lips touch, however briefly. It had been fatal; it had been a taste of forbidden fruit, and now that she had savoured it she wanted more. She sank down to her knees and closed her eyes. How could she go on living here now? What was she to do? How could they act naturally with this mountain looming between them?

It wasn't just the kiss, it was something more. They might as well have made love. It had been a savage declaration of their feelings which had risen from nowhere and taken them both over. A primeval act born of desperate hunger.

Cameron had never given any indication that he felt like this—unless, of course, she was reading more into it than there was? The thought shocked her to her senses. He was a healthy male animal, with a perfectly healthy male appetite. The urge had overtaken him and she was the only available female!

It needn't have been her, it could have been anyone. They had been together for several hours yesterday, and again this morning—it was a natural enough thing to happen, given the circumstances. No man could remain celibate forever, especially someone like Cameron.

Her kaleidoscope of feelings faded, leaving a strange, bitter taste in her mouth. It could have been anyone! The thought haunted her, and yet it was the most likely explanation. Cameron had emphatically declared that he never intended getting married, that he preferred this sort of life to domesticity, but that didn't stop him getting his pleasure when and where he could.

Julie shivered. She had come dangerously close to giving herself away; the fact that the kiss had been so short was her only saviour. Even then she hadn't rejected him. It was an insane situation and she should never have let it happen.

But she couldn't have been forewarned. It had taken

place so suddenly, so unexpectedly. They had been laughing like children over a foolish tale he'd told her, and then—wham—a kiss to surpass all kisses.

How could such a brief touch of his lips have done this to her? The answer was simple. It was what she had hungered for almost from their first meeting—and what she could never experience again. No matter what, she had to maintain the sham of her marriage to Ian. It would crucify her even more, now that her appetite had been whetted, but she could not let her brother down.

'Julie, are you all right?' It was Ian walking towards her, a towel over his arm, obviously with the same intention of using the lagoon. He dropped to his knees beside her and took her face between his palms. He saw the distress in her eyes and a frown grooved his brow.

'What's wrong now? Cameron came storming back a few moments ago and didn't even speak,' he said harshly. 'I had no idea that you were up; I thought you were still asleep. What on earth's going on?'

Julie shook her head, trying to look rueful, trying desperately hard to hide her real hurt. 'I guess your boss and me don't see eye to eye.'

Ian gave a groan, his hands slid to his sides, and she could see him wishing his job goodbye.

'But it's nothing too serious,' she assured him. 'It won't affect things here; I won't let it.'

'What were you arguing about this time?' he asked worriedly. 'Us again? Is he still asking questions? Maybe I've ignored things for too long. Maybe you're right and he does——'

'It wasn't that this time,' Julie cut in urgently. 'It was—nothing really. Just a personality clash. I promise you, Ian, I'll try not to rub him up the wrong way again.'

'I'd appreciate that, Sis.' He still looked excessively concerned. 'I'm going for a dip now. I'd like it if when I came back you two were friends.'

Julie nodded, not really knowing what else to do.

'How's your foot?'

'I'll live,' she acknowledged wryly.

'Can you walk?'

'Yes, thank you.'

He helped her to feet. 'I never expected you to hate Cameron. I know you've been anti-men for years, and I know Roger didn't help, but I did think that——'

'I don't hate him,' she interrupted swiftly and firmly.

His smile was weak. 'I wish I could believe you.'

'It's the truth. Ian. It really is.'

He looked into her eyes for a long, long time, and finally seemed satisfied. 'I'll see you later, Sis.'

Julie's footsteps got slower and slower as she limped back to camp. She was in dire pain, but more troubling still were thoughts of the reception she would get. What sort of mood would Cameron be in?

To her amazement, he was grilling sausages for their breakfast. His white trunks had been replaced by blue shorts and shirt, a tea-towel was tied around his waist and the inevitable mocking-birds were pecking around for scraps of food. He looked at Julie as she came up to him, his face impassive, with no glimmer of any sort of emotion.

'I can do the breakfast,' she said.

His eyes derided her. 'When your foot's better. Why don't you get dressed? Or is it your intention to put *more* temptation my way?'

He *was* blaming her! The sharpness of his words cut

deep and her eyes flashed. 'If you're insinuating that I asked for that kiss then you're far wide of the mark.'

'Am I?' Mocking brows lifted. 'If you didn't want the kiss why didn't you stop me? Something tells me that——'

Julie cut into his words furiously. 'Of course I didn't want you to kiss me. It's the last thing I'd want. And let me tell you this, *Mr* Storm, I do not think much of men who go around kissing married women.'

With that parting shot she spun on her heel and headed for the privacy of her tent. In her anger she forgot her foot. She put it to the ground and creased in agony as pressure on the wound sent a pain searing up her leg, stumbling as she recovered her balance, hurrying away as fast as her foot and her dignity would let her.

In her tent, she flopped down on her camp-bed. Tears filled her eyes. His kiss had unlocked the floodgates. How was she going to cope now?

# CHAPTER SEVEN

THE days that followed were some of the most uncomfortable Julie had ever spent. Cameron's kiss had triggered within her such violent emotions that it was difficult to keep them suppressed. One look at him had her stomach churning until she began to feel quite ill, and the times she relived the kiss were too numerous to count.

The one blessing was that he and Ian were out most of the time. An awning had been rigged over a make-shift desk and she began to type out Cameron's book. It made fascinating reading and some of his observations were extremely witty. It was a pity, she thought, that she rarely saw this side of him.

She swam in the lagoon whenever she got too hot, washed her clothes there—it made an ideal washing place because the tide changed the water twice a day—collected water from the still, which she then refrigerated, and sometimes simply sat watching the antics of the birds and the iguanas.

There was always something going on among the numerous fearless creatures which colonised the islands, and constantly she had to chase the sandy-coloured mocking-birds away from their food tent, their long legs carrying them along at astonishing speed.

It pleased her that Ian was content. He came back to their camp each evening tired but happy, and there was no repeat of his migraine. In this respect she had no regrets about coming out here.

Cameron, too, was in good humour. The kiss certainly wasn't on *his* conscience, and Julie thought she had done a good job of hiding her own feelings until one evening after supper, when Ian had gone to his tent to write up his notes. Cameron looked at her speculatively and said, 'You're not looking well, Julie.'

So far he had avoided personal issues. Ever since that eventful morning he had spoken only about his work and given her whatever instructions he felt necessary each day. Now, sitting together in the dusky night air, Julie felt a stirring of unease.

'I'm all right,' she answered, smiling brightly and, she hoped, convincingly.

'Is your foot still troubling you?'

'No.' she shook her head. 'Well, not much anyway.'

'Aren't you happy here? Is the island too quiet? Are you missing the company of others? If that is the case——he gave her no chance to deny it '—if you're hating it so much that you cannot hide your feelings, then I suggest you leave. I'll radio for the boat and you can return to England as soon as practical.' His blue eyes were intent on hers. 'Ian also, of course.'

His unexpected words hit her like an icy blast and Julie knew she had to be quick to rescue the situation. Ian would never forgive her if she spoilt things for him now. 'I never said I hated it.'

'Not in so many words.'

'But I don't,' she insisted. 'I like it here. It's different and interesting and—and I like it, I really do.'

Cameron's eyes narrowed and he looked at her for a long, thoughtful moment.

'There's something about these islands that has captured my imagination,' she added. 'I don't want to go home.'

'I admit you gave that impression the day I took you exploring,' he agreed. 'So it leaves only one other explanation for your attitude.'

Julie's heart hammered uncomfortably. He had obviously known all along what was the matter with her. 'How do you expect me to behave,' she asked brittly, 'after what you said? I object most strongly to you laying the blame for the kiss in my court. I certainly didn't invite it.'

'No?' he queried, eyes cruelly searching.

'Most definitely not.' Her chin came up.

'Maybe you did it unconsciously? Maybe you're so used to using your body for good effect that it's second nature? You're a highly dangerous lady, Julie Drummond. It's no wonder men are attracted to you.'

'I beg your pardon?' Such damning words! 'Highly dangerous' indeed! What was he talking about? She had never been guilty of being provocative in her life; it wasn't in her nature.

'Jake, for instance?' he rasped. 'And goodness knows how many others before. Are you ever true to one person, Julie? You admitted yourself that there had been others at the same time as you were going out with Ian.'

'I think you're crazy,' she said sharply. 'I think you're trying to cover up your own weakness.'

Blue eyes narrowed warningly. 'Weakness, Julie?'

'Yes, weakness,' she snapped. 'Only a man with no self-control would kiss a—a woman who isn't free.'

His mouth curved into a sneer. 'Or only a frustrated woman would kiss another man. Is sleeping in separate tents having a profound effect on you?'

'Of course not.' She sat a little bit straighter.

'Is that so?' he asked coolly, and with a certain amount of humour.

'We're—very discreet,' she told him.

'Really?' His lips twitched at the corners and Julie knew that he didn't believe a word she said.

She drew in a ragged sigh. If she had known how difficult it was all going to be she would certainly have had second thoughts about agreeing to Ian's suggestion. Not only second, but third and fourth as well. It was an impossible situation, becoming more and more volatile with each day that passed.

It was completely dark by now; the only light was from Ian's solar lamp. She observed his outline through the canvas and wondered what he would say if she told him that Cameron had asked questions about their love-life. Would he be equally as alarmed, or would he shrug that off the same as he had everything else?

Julie slept little that night and woke with heavy eyes and a feeling of desperation. A swim in the lagoon did nothing to help, and when Cameron met her coming back she was subjected to his critical gaze yet again.

'Another stolen night of love?' he taunted.

She flashed her eyes and said nothing, but she felt uncomfortable over breakfast, especially when he kept looking at her with that same amused expression on his face. Had he sat up all night and watched? Did he know that she hadn't moved out of her tent?

When the two men had gone she sat down and tried to recover her composure, wishing her own feelings were as still and untroubled as the calm waters of the bay. When a boat appeared she watched with interest, especially when it dropped anchor and a dinghy began to make its way slowly towards the shore.

At first she thought it was Jake, and her heart beat uneasily. She knew that Cameron would instantly assume it was because of her he had come back. But then she realised it wasn't *Sea Lady* at all, but another similar vessel, and as the dinghy got closer she could see that there was more than one person on board.

'Ahoy there!' shouted a cheerful young man, the first to jump ashore. 'We were told this island was uninhabited. Who are you, Girl Friday?'

Julie grinned. He was blond and fresh-faced, wearing nothing but a pair of denim cut-offs, his handsome body oiled and deeply tanned. 'My name's Julie,' she said. 'I'm with two others, scientists, doing some research on the island.'

He looked impressed. 'Do you mind if we come ashore?'

'Not at all,' she told him. There were three of them, two young men and a girl, all with blonde hair, all cheerful, and obviously thoroughly enjoying themselves.

But whereas Julie had expected them to stay for an hour or so and then depart, they actually announced their intention of setting up camp on the island.

'There's only this beach, I'm afraid,' Julie told them.

'That's all right, we'll take the other end,' said Rick, the one who had first spoken to her. He was sublimely unaware of the fact that he could be disturbing them. 'I bet you could do with some company.'

Julie got no typing done that day. Rick and Lee, who were brothers, invited her to join them, and Alex, their cousin, opened a bottle of wine. Julie could not help but like them. They were a friendly group, who welcomed her warmly into their midst.

Time passed so quickly that Cameron and Ian were back before she had even begun to prepare their evening meal.

Cameron's expression was thunderous when he saw their visitors, and Julie sitting chatting to them as if she had known them all her life. 'What's going on?' he demanded as he strode into their camp.

Julie sprang to her feet. 'This is Rick and——'

'I don't want to know who they are,' he bellowed, 'I want to know what they are doing here.'

'We're on holiday,' said Rick politely.

'In that case I'd be obliged if you'd go and holiday somewhere else.' Cameron stood tall and broad, and glowered down at the three younger people in his most intimidating manner. 'I trust you're aware of the fact that you cannot go tramping willy-nilly around these islands?'

'Indeed we are,' answered Rick, still with respect, and Julie admired his constraint. He was about twenty-five, very good-looking and almost six feet tall.

'Nor can you stay here,' insisted Cameron

Rick frowned. 'Why not?'

'Because we're here.'

'But the island's not private.'

'No,' admitted Cameron, 'but I like *my* privacy. I want you off here straight away. I have work to do.'

'I promise we'll keep to our end of the beach,' said Rick. 'We'll not get in your way.'

Cameron was left with no choice, but back in their own camp he said brusquely, 'What the hell were you doing, letting them come ashore?'

Julie looked at him in astonishment. 'How was I supposed to stop them?'

'You could have told them the island was private.'

'They knew it wasn't.'

'You could have said that visitors weren't welcome.'

'I could have said a lot of things,' she snapped, feeling that he was being unfair. 'But it was three against one. I didn't relish arguing with them.'

'Even so, you didn't have to be so friendly.'

'And why not?' He was being boorish about the whole thing. 'They're a nice bunch, easy to get on with.'

'So I noticed,' he commented bitterly. 'You had so much fun that you didn't give Ian or me a second thought. How long have they been here?'

'All day,' she admitted.

'So you've done nothing except sit and chat?' Dark brows rose accusingly.

'I didn't realise the time,' she confessed. 'I'll get our meal now. It won't take long.'

'I'm not talking about food, Julie. You're here to work, not fraternise with whoever takes it into their mind to invade the island. I realise I cannot stop anyone else arriving, but I do take exception to you spending so much time with them.'

'I was being polite.' She felt he was going too far, that he was making a bigger issue than was necessary. And it was a wonder he hadn't accused her of throwing herself at the young men. She could understand him being angry because their meal wasn't ready—they were always starving when they came back—but a few hours out of her week to chat to their visitors was surely nothing to argue about.

Ian looked at them both questioningly as they returned. 'Who are they?'

'Just holidaymakers,' answered Julie.

'Troublemakers,' growled Cameron.

And later that evening, when Rick, Lee and Alex walked across and invited them over for a drink, Julie thought Cameron was going to explode. It became very clear that he did not like intruders, that he preferred to choose his own companions, and they did not include strangers who had invaded his privacy.

'I do not imbibe while I am working,' he replied caustically. 'If you must camp on this beach then so be it, but I'd be obliged if you'd keep yourselves to yourselves.'

The two brothers looked at each other and shrugged, but the girl could not keep her eyes off Cameron. Whether it was his fantastic physique or his powerful magnetism that attracted her, Julie was not sure, but, whatever, she was totally fascinated.

Cameron himself did not notice; he was too busy blasting them to see that Alex was gazing adoringly at him. But Lee noticed and he frowned, tugging at his cousin's arm. 'Come on, let's go,' he muttered. 'I knew it was a dumb idea anyway.'

The three sauntered back to their camp, the girl still looking occasionally over her shoulder. She was a leggy blonde and very beautiful, and Julie was glad Cameron hadn't noticed how pretty she was. She could not have stood it had he shown an interest in her.

The whole evening was a disaster. Cameron hardly spoke, Julie and Ian chatted desultorily, and from the opposite end of the beach came the sound of music and laughter. And the louder the laughter the more thunderous became Cameron's expression.

Even after they had gone to bed the noise did not abate, and it was well after midnight before their visitors settled down.

When she awoke the next morning at daybreak and poked her head out of the tent Julie could not believe her eyes when she saw Cameron and Alex swimming together in the ocean. The young girl wore a white swimsuit that had turned almost diaphanous in the water, and was posing and cavorting and showing Cameron in the most blatant way possible that she was interested in him.

And Cameron, to Julie's amazement, was responding. He seemed not to mind. In fact, he looked flattered by the girl's attention. Unable to bear the pain of seeing them together, Julie dodged back into her tent— and it was at that moment it struck her that she was in love with Cameron! This was why it hurt so much.

All the feelings she had thought were purely physical were much more than that. It was her emotions that were involved, her heart—and at this moment it felt as though it was in danger of breaking in two.

Usually each morning she bathed in the lagoon, but now she did not want to leave her tent, at least not until the two of them had finished playing. Her ears were keenly attuned. Alex's laughter floated on the air, light and carefree; she was thoroughly enjoying herself, and occasionally Cameron's own bark of laughter sounded in response. It was as though he too was throwing caution to the winds. Gone was the serious side of him, in its place boyish good humour, something she herself had glimpsed only occasionally.

Was that what it took? A much younger girl? Or someone free and unattached? Had she ruined any chance whatsoever of Cameron relaxing with her in such a manner by assuming the role of Ian's wife?

Finally, after what seemed like forever, they came out of the water. Julie heard them talking, heard their feet crunching on the crushed coral beach, and she half expected Cameron to invite the girl to stay for breakfast. But no, one set of footsteps continued into the distance, until finally all was silent again.

It was obvious that Rick and Lee had slept through it all, Ian too, and Julie decided it was best to pretend that she had not seen them either. She waited a decent half-hour before donning her swimsuit and heading for the lagoon, and she could not believe it when Cameron joined her.

Last night he had been in a black mood, this morning he was light-hearted and cheerful. What was she supposed to think? She decided to test him. 'You look happier this morning. Is it because you're hoping our visitors will leave?'

'That's up to them, isn't it?' he said, much to her surprise.

Julie swallowed hard. It could only be because of Alex that he had changed his mind. She felt a sharp stab of disappointment, as though a knife had pierced her heart.

'How about you, Julie, do you want our intruders to leave? Or are they just the diversion you need? Another couple of healthy red-blooded males to dig your talons into?'

This was an unprecedented attack and Julie's eyes shot sparks of fire. 'You bastard!'

'You're still protesting your love for Ian?'

'Of course I am,' she tossed haughtily.

'But how deep is that love?' he derided. 'What sort of love is it?'

'The sort to stop me playing around with someone else,' she snapped. And that was the truth. She loved her brother dearly, and while she was masquerading as his wife she would never do anything to jeopardise his job, even though it meant something as soul-destroying as hiding her love for Cameron.

It was such a new and wondrous discovery, and such a tragedy that she had to keep it to herself. She couldn't even tell Ian because he would be overcome with remorse; he would blame himself for spoiling her life.

Not that anything would ever come of it, even if they confessed their deception. Cameron didn't love her, he loved his job. He might have amused himself with her, the same as with Alex, but that wasn't what she wanted.

As soon as they reached the lagoon she slipped into the water. Cameron sat on the edge and watched. 'Why don't you come in?' she called, feeling it would be preferable to this slow, thoroughly disturbing appraisal.

'I've already had my morning swim,' he told her, but he did not mention that he'd had company and Julie wondered whether it was a deliberate omission.

'There's nothing to stop you coming in again.'

'I'm enjoying watching you.'

Just as you enjoyed romping with Alex, she thought bitterly. The pool was deep following the earlier tide and she dived to the bottom, sharing the pleasure with dozens of tiny fish, wishing passionately that Cameron would go away. The more time they spent together now the worse it was going to be. But wishing made no difference. He was still there when she resurfaced, still watching her just as intently, still tearing her heart apart.

He took her hand and helped her out, and it was as though she had grabbed hold of a hot iron—heat and passion searing through her, destroying her, making her tug away as soon as she was safely over the jagged rocks.

Intent only on escape, Julie missed Cameron's frown, the tightening of muscles in his jaw, the sudden calculating gleam in his eyes. Her feelings were getting more intense by the day, by the hour, by the minute— even by the second. She could foresee the time when she would be unable to keep her new-found love hidden—and that would be disastrous.

Over breakfast Cameron was once again quiet, and after they had finished he surprised Julie by sending Ian off by himself while he went to talk to their visitors.

Julie cleared away and sat down to type, but it was impossible to concentrate. Her gaze kept wandering to the other end of the beach, and although she was too far away to hear their conversation she could see Cameron and Alex deep in conversation.

It was a good half-hour before he returned, and she saw the three young people disappear over the rocks in the opposite direction. 'I've told our neighbours how important your work is,' he said, 'and that they're not to disturb you. I trust you'll catch up today?'

Julie looked at him in astonishment. 'One day I've had off. What kind of a monster are you?'

'I expect perfection,' he answered coolly.

'And you get it,' she riposted.

'You let me down.'

'It won't happen again.'

'It had better not.'

His attitude really got to her, and before she could stop herself Julie said, 'It's all right for you to play around with Alex, but I have to work like a slave and keep myself to myself. Is that what you're saying?'

Dark brows rose reprovingly. 'My, my, we are touchy this morning. Suppose you tell me what are you talking about?'

'I saw you swimming.'

'Is that so?' He looked surpised. 'Why didn't you join us?'

'Because you seemed to be having *such* a good time,' she answered sarcastically. 'I didn't think my company would be welcome.'

His lips suddenly and amazingly twitched. 'That sounds like sour grapes. I wonder why me enjoying myself with another girl should upset a married woman like you?'

Julie saw disaster with a capital D looming. 'Of course I'm not bothered,' she responded quickly. 'It's just that you made such a big thing about them invading your privacy that it struck me as being rather peculiar.'

His mouth widened into a smile. 'She's actually quite a nice girl, when you get to know her. She's fun. I think she'll be quite an amusing diversion.' And with that surprising statement he made his way towards the cliffs.

Diversion! Julie felt tears close to the surface. Damn! How could she sit and watch him playing around with Alex, feeling as she did? It would be pure, unadulterated torture.

She sat down at her typewriter, but it was a full minute before she recalled that the day before yesterday she had come to a full stop because she couldn't read his handwriting. Usually she had no problem, but in this particular instance she could not decipher it at all.

'Cameron,' she called, springing to her feet. 'Cameron!' Perhaps she could catch up with him before he went too far, or at least get within shouting distance.

But whether it was because she was hurrying, or whether it was because she was not so sure-footed as Cameron, who had climbed the cliffside as nimbly as a goat, she was less than halfway up when her foot slipped, and before she could save herself she went crashing and rolling all the way back to the bottom, feeling each bump on the way, feeling as though every bone in her body was being broken.

When she tried to call out nothing happened; every bit of breath was knocked out of her. More than a minute went by before she was able to make any sound. 'Cameron!' Her voice was faint at first, then gathered strength. '*Cameron*! Cameron! Help! Help me, Cameron.'

# CHAPTER EIGHT

JULIE began to think that Cameron had not heard her calls, that she would have to get up and lick her own wounds. She prayed nothing was broken. And then she heard his voice, faintly at first but getting louder. 'Julie, did you call? Julie, what's wrong? Where are you?'

'Down here.' Her voice was fragile. She felt faint now, with the pain and the discomfort and the heat. There seemed not one part of her body that did not hurt.

In no time he had reached her and his face was full of concern. 'What happened?' he asked as he immediately and expertly began to feel for broken bones.

'I was coming after you,' she said huskily, 'and I fell, and, oh, God, it hurts.' It was with great difficulty that she held back the tears.

'You could have broken your back,' he muttered, his face serious with concentration as he felt her limbs and then raised and bent each leg and arm in turn. 'I've trained for all sorts of emergencies,' he reassured her. 'You can't afford to be complacent when you live like this for many months of the year. Tell me if anywhere hurts unduly.'

Julie winced suddenly. 'Yes, it hurts when you move my right arm, and it hurts to breathe as well. Just here.' She touched her side with her other hand and Cameron frowned.

'Here?' He felt her ribs with his fingertips, concentrating, watching her face for any reaction.

She nodded, wincing as he found the spot.

'I think you've possibly cracked a rib or two,' he told her sympathetically. 'Did you hit your side as you fell?'

Julie nodded. 'I remember banging it on the edge of a boulder. It winded me for a second or two.'

'It would,' he agreed, 'and it's going to hurt for quite a long time. Let's get you back and I'll give you something to ease the pain.'

He lifted her up, ignoring her suggestion that she could walk, and once again she was held against his hard, dynamic body; once again she felt the destroying maleness of him. On top of that she felt foolish; he must think she was accident-prone. Twice in a few days she had hurt herself, and this time it would take much longer to recover. She was not going to be much use to him. Probably this time he *would* send her home. And even in the depths of her pain the thought caused her despair.

He gave her painkillers and made her comfortable, putting her camp-bed beneath the awning where she usually sat and typed, plumping pillows behind her because it hurt to lie flat, and even when she said she was all right he did not leave; he sat by her on a chair and looked as though he was prepared to stay all day long.

'I'm sorry,' she said. 'I seem to be making a habit of doing stupid things. If you want to send me back home I'll understand.'

'Accidents happen,' he said, with surprising understanding. 'What was so important that it wouldn't wait?'

'I couldn't read your writing.'

'Is that all?' he asked with a genuine laugh.

'It was holding me up.'

'And you thought I'd be cross if you didn't get on with my book?'

'Well, wouldn't you?' she asked.

His generous lips twisted into a rueful smile. 'I guess I would; I can't bear slacking in anyone. But now you've got your own back. You won't be able to work today after all.'

It was Julie's turn to smile wryly, self-consciously. 'I'm sorry. I know how important it is that you get this book finished.'

His answering smile was gentle and compassionate. 'I'm sure you'll catch up once you're feeling better. It wasn't your fault you fell.'

He was being so nice to her that it hurt. If only he could be like this all the time. Why did they have to argue? Why was he hard on her? At least it proved he did have a caring side. It was worth breaking her ribs to find that out.

'You've fitted in much better than I expected, Julie,' he said, much to her surprise. 'Some women have hated it out here.'

'I guess Ian's enthusiasm has rubbed off on me.'

'Ian!' he exclaimed. 'Of course, you must want him with you. Will you be all right while I go and——?'

'It doesn't matter,' cut in Julie firmly. 'Don't disturb him. He enjoys himself out there. Don't spoil his day.'

Cameron's brows lifted. 'You think he wouldn't want to come, if he knew?'

'Of course he would,' she said at once, 'but he can't do anything, can he?' And then, as another thought struck her, 'I'm being selfish, aren't I? You want to get back to work yourself. I'm sorry. Please, it's all right, you go. Tell Ian if you like. Otherwise I'll be all right by myself.'

'The hell you will,' he growled. 'If you really don't want me to fetch Ian then of course I'll stay. I can write, I can do other things, or I can sit here with you,' he added, with a smile that did turbulent things to her heart.

And so he stayed. They spent the whole day together—Julie resting on her bed, Cameron waiting on her, fixing their lunch, preparing the evening meal, his eyes rarely off her for more than a few seconds at a time.

Rick and the others came back from their trek over the island and were extremely concerned when they heard of her accident. 'If there's anything we can do. . .' Rick said.

'Anything at all,' purred Alex, but her eyes were on Cameron and not on Julie.

When Ian returned he was naturally distressed. 'Why on earth didn't you let me know, Cameron?'

He pulled a face. 'Ask Julie. It was her choice. She didn't want you to be disturbed.'

Ian frowned. 'Why ever not?' He dropped to his knees and took her hand, looking desperately worried.

Julie smiled self-consciously. 'What good would it have done? Cameron's looked after me; I couldn't have asked for a better nurse.'

'I've been called some things in my time,' grunted Cameron good-humouredly

'You know what I mean,' she said, and it felt good, the rapport they now shared.

The only bad part about the situation was Alex at the other end of the beach. She sauntered over again later in the evening, and she and Cameron spent over an hour laughing and talking.

Julie did not sleep well that night. It was agony to

move in any direction, but more than that she was troubled by thoughts of Cameron and Alex. He couldn't have made his interest in this stunning, long-legged blonde more clear.

Again, at daybreak, they went swimming together. Julie did not see them, but she heard Alex's excited voice, and she began to think that it might be a good idea if she did go home. There was only a certain amount of this she could take.

Ian helped her get out of bed in time for breakfast, and once she was on her feet the pain in her ribs wasn't so bad; however, the pain in her heart refused to go away.

The two men were debating who should stay with her when yet another boat headed into the harbour. It dropped anchor and the usual dinghy made its way steadily towards them.

Julie looked at Cameron, expecting him to show further resentment at yet another intrusion into their privacy, but instead he was watching the dinghy with interest. There was only one man in it.

When he reached the shore and climbed out Julie felt her heart drop into her shoes. She tried to tell herself it wasn't happening. That it was a dream, a nightmare. But it wasn't. The man who came walking towards them was a very familiar figure indeed.

Cameron extended his hand. 'It's good to see you, Roger.'

'You too.' The newcomer was tall and slim with sandy hair and green eyes and he looked as shocked to see Julie as she was to see him. 'You didn't tell me that you had these two working for you, Cameron. I know them well; we were once virtually neighbours. What a surprise, meeting again like this.'

A surprise, indeed, thought Julie. He had accused her of two-timing him, he had broken her heart and made her so miserable that she had never thought to be happy again, and she definitely wasn't pleased to see him now.

Ian was equally as agitated and he glanced at his sister in concern, putting his arm reassuringly about her shoulders. 'What are you doing here, Roger?' He unconsciously voiced the question that was troubling her also.

Roger smiled widely and happily. 'Cameron's invitation—what else? He and I go back a long way. Is your wife here, my friend?'

Cameron's invitation! To confirm his suspicions! To force the issue! He had somehow known that Roger was their friend also. There was a silence so loud that it hurt Julie's ears. Ian's arm tightened around her and she dared not look at Cameron. She wished the floor would open and swallow her up—swallow them both up.

'I'm afraid not,' muttered her brother uncomfortably.

'She didn't fancy the idea of coming out here?'

'Something like that.'

'And so your faithful twin came instead. Aren't they enchanting islands, Julie?' He gave no indication that they had parted on bad terms.

'Very much so,' she agreed quietly.

Roger suddenly seemed to realise that something wasn't quite as it should be. He looked at each of them in turn, a frown of puzzlement on his face. 'Have I said something wrong?'

'Am I right in believing,' asked Cameron, his voice dangerously quiet, 'that this is not Ian's wife?'

'Of course she's not his wife,' said Roger in bewilderment. They're twins, and very close twins, I might add; they were hardly ever separated before Julie came on the scene.'

'Julie being Ian's wife, his *real* wife?' questioned Cameron.

'Confusing, isn't it, both of them having the same name?' asked Roger, smiling weakly now, unable to work out what was wrong.

Julie wanted to die. She was right to have been worried. This really was the end. Cameron looked positively murderous.

'I trust you have a very good reason for this duplicity?' Cameron looked straight at her as he spoke, his tone so hard and condemning that she felt as though she was being whiplashed. The air positively crackled.

'It was my idea,' said Ian hastily, swallowing hard, looking desperately worried also. 'My wife and I are—er—separated.'

'Was that any reason to lie?' demanded Cameron. His blue eyes had turned an icy grey, blasting Ian now with their coldness.

'I thought that you—er—wouldn't give me the job if you knew.'

'And so, between you, you devised a little scheme to delude me into believing that you were husband and wife? Julie?' His head snapped in her direction, his eyes sharp on her as he spoke.

'I can't see that it matters all that much,' she said in a brave, strong voice, feeling the need to try and protect her brother. 'You admit I'm efficient,

Cameron. Ian's doing his job successfully. Why is our being married so important?'

His eyes glittered his impatience. 'Hell, the job doesn't matter; I'd have given it to you anyway if you'd asked. It's the lies I abhor—the deception, the fraud. You attempted to make a fool of me, dammit.'

'That wasn't our intention,' said Ian, his face still anxious.

'I'm sure it wasn't,' put in Roger politely.

Julie gave him a wan, thankful smile, but Cameron threw him a look of extreme intolerance. 'We'll continue this conversation some other time. Ian, you go and carry on with your work. Julie, make yourself scarce. Roger, thank you for coming. How about a drink?'

Julie could not get over the fact that Cameron had actually invited Roger here. Did he also know that Roger had been her boyfriend? About his accusations? Did he know everything? She glanced worriedly at Ian and he looked wretched also, but he gave her a further reassuring hug before striding away to do as he was bidden.

Julie went into her tent and lay down, a hundred questions crowding into her mind at once. What would their future hold now? Would Cameron send them both home? Was this the end of Ian's hopes and aspirations? She felt so sorry for him, so sad, so extremely sad. It almost outweighed her own problems.

Although it was a relief that the truth was out, any chance of something growing between her and Cameron had been ruined because of their lies. If only Ian had been honest from the beginning. If only she hadn't gone along with his brainless idea. If only, if only. . .

Roger came to find her an hour later. 'I never thought we'd meet again like this, Julie.'

'Neither did I,' she said with a wry twist to her lips. What had happened between her and Roger seemed of no consequence compared to this latest tragedy.

'For what it's worth, I didn't mean to spoil your little game.'

She lifted her shoulders. 'I think Cameron already knew.'

'And I was called in to confirm it,' he added ruefully. 'Actually, lying to Cameron was the worst thing either of you could have done. He cannot tolerate lies.'

Julie sighed unhappily. 'I guess this is the end for me and Ian.'

'Perhaps he'll calm down,' said Roger, though she could see he did not really believe it.

He was silent for a few moments, deep in thought, and then he looked at her and said, 'In one way I'm thankful to Cameron for bringing me out here, because it's given me the opportunity to put matters straight.'

How could he ever hope to do that after the things he had said, the claims he had made? Didn't he know how much he had hurt her?

'I want to apologise, Julie.' His green eyes were imploring on hers. 'I gave you a hard time, and I was wrong. I discovered that later. I was totally wrong, totally out of order. You were telling the truth when you said there was nothing between you and Tod Martin.'

Her eyes flashed at him cynically. 'Of course I was. I never lie.' And then she realised what she had said and gave an embarrassed laugh.

He looked at her long and hard and said hopefully, 'I guess it's too late to put back the clock?'

If Julie hadn't been hurting so much from her ribs, and if she hadn't been feeling so desolate over her and Ian's deception, she would have told him to get lost. Instead she smiled weakly. 'I'm afraid so, Roger.'

'I've ruined my chances?'

'Yes.'

He grimaced ruefully. 'It's a pity. I was a fool not to trust you. You're a wonderful girl, Julie. Some man's going to be very lucky.' Again there was silence between them, each deep in their own thoughts.

Julie knew she would never get married now. Cameron was the only man she wanted and she would rather remain single than settle for second-best.

'Cameron's asked me to stay over,' said Roger at length, 'but I don't think so. It wouldn't be fair on you and me, for one thing. I'll go back to Santa Cruz; I'm staying there for a while. I guess I've been an unwitting pawn in your game. You and Cameron will have a lot of talking to do.'

All the talking in the world wouldn't mend matters, Julie thought dismally. It wouldn't excuse the lies and the deceit. 'Help me up,' she said, 'and I'll come and see you off.'

He willingly gave her his arm. 'Cameron said you'd cracked a couple of ribs. Hard luck. I bust some myself a few years ago, I know how painful it is.'

But not so unrelenting as the pain in her heart, thought Julie.

'Can I have one last kiss, for old times' sake?' he asked with a pleading smile.

He took her carefully into his arms and his kiss was gentle and apologetic, and then Alex came into their camp. Julie had no choice but to introduce them, and it amused her to see what an impact she made on Roger. He could not take his eyes off her.

She was the sort of girl who flirted with any new male, but it was to Cameron she turned once Roger had headed back to his dinghy. Julie resumed her seat beneath the awning and shortly afterwards Alex, dismissed by Cameron, returned to her own end of the beach.

'Why, Julie? Why?' Cameron stood looking tightly down at her, his face hard and unreadable. 'Why wasn't I told the truth?'

She grimaced and shifted uneasily in her seat. 'Ian thought he wouldn't get the job, and he really was desperate to come out here. It's something he's always wanted to do. Charles Darwin is his hero and——'

'That hasn't answered my question,' he cut in sharply.

'Ian thought you wouldn't entertain his application if you knew that he and his wife were separated.' Julie tried to keep her voice level. Arguing with Cameron now would make matters even worse—if that were possible!

'I wouldn't have been happy,' he agreed. 'Lord, he hadn't been married five minutes. What went wrong?'

'She ran off with his best friend,' answered Julie unhappily. 'He still loves her, though, and he'd have her back tomorrow if there was half a chance.'

Cameron grunted. 'Does no marriage ever last? What is wrong with everyone?'

Julie knew he was thinking of his parents, as she frequently did of her own. It was a sad world. But she wasn't prepared when he thumped his fist on the table in front of her. She jumped, jarring her ribs painfully as she did so.

'It's the deception I find intolerable.'

'I'm sorry,' she whispered.

'Apologising doesn't put matters right,' he rasped, his eyes savage on hers.

It was difficult to believe that only yesterday, earlier this morning, even, he had been a different man. The compassion in him, his gentleness, his kindness, his very real concern, had warmed her through and through. Now she felt chilled to the very marrow.

'Did Ian really think I wouldn't find out?'

Julie nodded.

'He's an idiot; you didn't even behave like lovers. I actually knew before you got here that you weren't his wife.'

Julie's eyes popped wide. 'You did?'

'One hears a lot of things through the grapevine. Ian should be careful who he speaks to.'

'And yet you didn't say. I don't understand.'

'I thought I'd play along with your little masquerade,' he told her brutally, 'see what sort of a mess you got yourselves into. I think it was Sir Walter Scott who said, "O what a tangled web we weave, When first we practise to deceive!". I've enjoyed seeing you squirm, Julie.'

She closed her eyes, unable to look at him, not wanting to see the cruel anger on his face.

'Have you nothing to say for yourself?'

'What can I say?' she asked in a miserable whisper.

'Indeed,' came the harsh response. 'And not only that, I've had to put up with someone who doesn't think twice about amusing herself with more than one man at a time.'

Her head jerked. 'What are you accusing me of now?' She was totally confused.

Blue eyes gleamed maliciously. 'Roger told me the whole story, long before I even gave Ian the job. He was bitterly humiliated, not to say jealous. He had to talk to someone and I happened to be there. Oh, yes, I knew all about Ian's sister.' His lip curled derisively as he spoke, and Julie wanted to crawl under her chair.

Nor was she given a chance to defend herself. 'And let me tell you this, *Miss* Julie Drummond,' he went on, his tone bitterly acrimonious, 'if I had known about this little deception before you left England, then I sure as hell wouldn't have given you the job.'

'Nor Ian?' she asked wretchedly.

He shook his head in exasperation. 'If he'd been honest in the beginning he would have got it; there's no doubt about that.' His eyes lashed her with their hardness. 'Why the hell he thought it necessary to devise a cock-and-bull story like this, I'll never know.'

Julie found the whole situation deeply discomfiting. She knew he had strongly suspected, but she had never been sure. She felt such a fool now.

'Besides,' he went on brusquely, 'you and Ian look alike. There's no mistaking that you're brother and sister.'

'No, we don't,' insisted Julie.

'Oh, yes, you do,' he returned, 'from certain angles. It's the jaw mainly, and the occasional expression. Why on earth did you go along with his insane suggestion?'

'Because I love him.'

'Not many sisters would do that.' There was grudging admiration in his voice.

His anger seemed to be abating, he was beginning to sound quite reasonable, and she felt faintly hopeful, but it lasted for no more than a few moments. He swung away, and when he turned back his eyes blazed out of a face that was set like a mask.

'I can accept that Ian's marriage has failed, Julie; I don't hold that against him. But I cannot accept the lies, the attempted deception. I have waited, with remarkable patience considering the circumstances, for you to tell me the truth.'

He paced up and down in front of her as he spoke, his whole body projecting his outrage. 'The fact that I had to get Roger out here to actually bring things to a head makes me very angry indeed. It makes me wonder what type of a person you are. Have you no integrity?'

'Ian wanted the job so desperately,' she whispered, all her pain showing in her face.

'Then it's a pity he didn't stop to think twice about the consequences of such an imbecilic action,' he rasped. 'And a pity that you didn't knock some sense into him. I have reached the limit of my patience, Julie. I have finally had enough of the pair of you.' His eyes were damning, cutting her down to the lowest of the low. 'I am, of course, sending you both home.'

Julie gasped, her eyes wide and disturbed. She had expected it, but even so the shock was numbing.

'Naturally, I realise that you're in no fit state to travel, and there is the fact that I need my book finished by the end of the month. You've proved yourself indispensable in that direction, so there is a respite. But make no bones about it,' he grated, 'the two of you leave here immediately after that.'

What could she say? Julie looked down at her hands, twisting the ring she had bought for the deception.

'Another give-away,' derided Cameron shortly. 'It's not the first time you've done that. A woman who has been married for almost two years would not play with her ring. She would be used to it. If you want to play games, Julie, then you should take the time to learn the rules.'

'Ian will be devastated,' she said. 'Can't you reconsider?'

His eyes flashed scornfully. 'Your brother should have thought of that before plotting such deceit.'

'But does it really make any difference?' she pleaded.

Cameron looked at her coldly. 'Not as far as work goes.'

'Then why can't you——?'

'I've told you why,' he grated. 'Now let that be an end to it. Can you manage if I go and find Ian? There are things I have to say to that young man.'

'Yes,' she said, her voice little more than a whisper.

It was the end of her dreams, the end of everything. Soon, all too soon, she would be back home in England—Ian too. And they would have nowhere to live because their house had been let for the next twelve months, and she would never see again the man that she loved. What a mess everything was all of a sudden.

She tried to type but it was impossible, far too painful yet to sit and work. She spent her time thinking, occasionally walking, sitting on the edge of the lagoon and dangling her feet into it, but she could see no way out of the situation.

Discovery had been her biggest nightmare and now it had happened. Cameron had reacted exactly as she had thought he would. Ian's confidence that he would never find out had been sadly misplaced. Why, oh why, had she ever agreed to such a lunatic idea?

Despite the considerable pain she was in every time

she moved, Julie managed to prepare their evening meal. She had actually expected Cameron back long before this; she had not thought he would spend the whole day with Ian, not after what had happened.

When the two men appeared Cameron's face was still grim, and he disappeared immediately inside his tent. Ian, looking extremely unhappy, sought Julie out. 'I'm sorry this had to happen, Sis.'

'Have you managed to persuade him to change his mind?'

Her brother shook his head. 'I've apologised over and over again, I've virtually grovelled at his feet, but it's made no difference. The man's adamant. Lord, I was a fool, thinking I could get away with it. If only I'd been honest with him. It was only because I mentioned I was married that he suggested Julie came too. I somehow got hold of the wrong idea, and now I've ruined everything.'

Cameron emerged from his tent, wearing black swimming-trunks, but he did not glance once in their direction as he headed for the lagoon. Julie looked sadly after him.

Ian caught her expression and frowned. 'There's something more, isn't there? There *is*! I've been blind. You're in love with the guy, aren't you?'

Julie nodded, her large hazel eyes swimming with unshed tears.

'Oh, lord.' Ian sat down on one of the collapsible canvas chairs and dropped his head into his hands. 'What a mess. What a complete and utter mess. My brave, dear sister, how could I not have noticed? You've had to suffer in silence because you were supposed to be my wife.'

'Ian, it doesn't matter.' She came towards him and

put her hand on his shoulder. 'Cameron doesn't feel that way about me, so nothing would have come of it, even without the pretence.'

He turned pained, glazed eyes in her direction. 'How can you be so sure?'

'Because I am,' she told him firmly. 'I've spent a lot of time with him. I can assure you I would have known if he felt anything.'

Ian shook his head. 'It doesn't matter. I still feel the world's biggest louse. I wouldn't hurt you for the world, Sis, you know that.'

'I know,' she said soothingly. 'And I'll get over him, don't worry.'

Over dinner there was complete and utter silence. It was the most uncomfortable meal Julie had ever experienced. She and Ian hardly touched their food. Cameron ate as normal, though his expression was anything but normal. A black scowl constantly darkened his brow, his eyes were unreadable, his mouth grim, his whole body rigid.

As soon as he had finished eating he disappeared, and when darkness fell Julie went to her tent and lay down. She did not get undressed, it was far too early to go to bed, but she needed to be alone; she wanted to listen to no more of Ian's apologies, feel no more of Cameron's animosity.

Finally she did get up and into her cotton nightshirt, but she was unable to sleep. Her mind was too tormented and her body aching, both from the pain in her ribs and the pain in her heart. She did not know which was the worst.

She left her tent open so that she could see the night sky, see the stars that looked down on them and the restless ocean that crept almost to their door during the night and then receded again.

When a black shape appeared she knew it was Ian, come to voice his misery again. 'Can't you sleep either?' she asked.

'You damnable woman,' growled a deep voice that definitely did not belong to her brother. 'You must know I can't sleep.' And with those pulsing words Cameron came into her tent.

# CHAPTER NINE

JULIE was trapped. Her injured ribs prevented her from moving—quickly enough anyway. It was agony even to lift herself into a sitting position. 'What do you want?' she asked, amazed to hear how husky her voice sounded. Almost like an invitation instead of panic! Her heart thudded wildly, every pulse raced, and she wished she could see Cameron's face. Only his voice told her that he was still in a foul mood.

'My retribution,' he growled, looming threateningly over her in the darkness.

'What do you mean?' She put a hand to her throat, sensing suddenly that she was in danger. This man had never posed a threat before, except to her own sanity, but now there was something different about him and she felt afraid.

He knelt down at her side, sitting back on his heels, though it was still impossible to see his face. 'Don't you know how difficult it has been for me to keep my hands off you?'

Julie swallowed a sudden lump in her throat. 'No— I——'

'You're too damned attractive for your own good, do you know that?' He leaned closer towards her, and now Julie could see the menacing glitter in his eyes. He looked as though something had snapped in his mind, and she feared all of a sudden for her safety.

'Cameron!' She tried to edge away, but there was nowhere to go. 'What is this? What are you——?'

'What am I trying to do?' he asked for her. 'Isn't it clear? You wanted me the moment you set eyes on me, and if it hadn't been for your admirable loyalty to your brother you would have undoubtedly let me see it. I intend only to take what you want to give.' There was a cruel quirk to his lips. 'It would be a shame to let you go without satisfying your hunger.'

Julie could not believe he was saying these things, and was appalled that he had been able to see through her so clearly. She felt abject humiliation and shook her head in a desperate attempt to deny his words. 'I don't, I don't,' she cried. 'You have it wrong. I've never felt like that about you. I——'

'Let's prove it, shall we?' he muttered against her mouth, relentlessly stemming her words.

She could not push him away, she could not struggle without causing herself severe pain and distress, and he knew it—knew she would be at his mercy. He had chosen his moment well.

His mouth took hers with such force that her head fell back. It was like an invasion of her deepest privacy, attacking the very roots of her womanhood.

One other kiss he had given her, one other kiss which had proved torment beyond compare, but even that meant nothing now. She could not breathe, her whole body trembled, the heat of unfulfilled passion rising like a flash-flood in her veins.

She was alarmed by her reaction and put her hands against his chest, but it hurt too much to push him away. Instead she felt the exciting heat of his bare skin pulsing against her palms, the silkiness of the dark hairs covering it, the powerful rhythm of his heart that echoed in frantic union with her own. It was like a pagan drumbeat, insistent, inciting passions, drumming inside her head as his mouth continued its assault.

His hands moved on her body, exploring, caressing, and there was nothing, but nothing she could do to stop him. Every movement she made caused pain. She was at his mercy, trapped in a confusion of feelings and sensations that threatened her very sanity.

Her breathing grew deep and ragged, her lips parting beneath his insistent invasion, a moan involuntarily escaping the back of her throat. It was sweet, sweet torture. Her whole body pulsed with excitement; she wanted to arch herself into him, take everything he had to offer, all thought of resistance fading like a rainbow after a shower.

The thud of her heart was painful in the extreme. So long she had loved this man and been unable to do anything about it; his kiss now was a release from her self-imposed torture, and although she knew she ought to pretend indifference it was impossible to control her snowballing feelings.

He lifted his mouth from hers and she drew in a much needed breath of air, but he had not finished with her. His lips continued to explore the rest of her face—her eyes, her nose, an incredibly erotic spot behind her ears—and Julie found herself moving her hips in a gesture of longing and needing, the pain from her ribs forgotten in the heat of desire.

She had slid back down the bed and his mouth now beat a torturous trail down the exposed column of her throat, his tongue tasting her skin, finding the erratic, tell-tale pulse in its hollow, his silence adding to the torment of the moment.

When his hand slid beneath her short cotton night-shirt to cup the soft curve of her breast Julie gave a gasp of unexpected pleasure, at the same time making a belated attempt to push him away.

'You want this, Julie, as much as I do,' he muttered thickly, his mouth against hers again. 'Deny it if you dare.'

How could she? It was torture of the sweetest kind. It was her dreams come true, even though she knew that he was using her in anger rather than pleasure, that he was taking rather than giving.

It was pain, but of the sweetest kind. This was an experience she would remember for a long time, long after she had left the islands, long after Cameron had forgotten all about her. She would never forget him, though. It was a cliché, but he was the man she had been waiting for all her life, and, had circumstances been different, the same might have gone for their relationship.

A ragged sigh lingered on her lips and Cameron took this as her answer. Her nightshirt was pushed up to expose to his glittering gaze the tautness of her breasts, nipples hard and thrusting, revealing all too clearly the full extent of her arousal.

Fingertips sought and teased, peaking her desire. Every pulse in her body was frantic, her heart crashing against her ribcage. Oh, lord, she wanted him. Never had she experienced such intense sensations, never had she hungered for a man like she did now for Cameron.

And when his mouth replaced his hands on her breasts, when his tongue and teeth gently tortured, she whimpered her pleasure, moaned with the exquisite pain of longing and wanting and needing that was a totally new experience.

She felt his deep, uneven breathing, the trembling of his body, and could not understand it when, with a cry of distaste, he jerked himself away. Her hands fluttered tentatively to stop him, but to no avail.

He stood looking down at her, his face harshly, savagely angular. 'Thank your lucky stars I'm too much of a gentleman to take complete advantage,' he rasped.

Julie's breathing was still heavy, sounding loud even to her own ears, and the blood pumped painfully through her veins as she lay watching him, her eyes wide and confused.

He had said he wanted retribution, but it hadn't felt like that—it had felt as though it meant something to him too. Yet now he was declaring it had all been a game, that it had been his intention to destroy her but he was going to be lenient and let her off.

Sweet pain turned to anger, erupting violently as she tugged her nightshirt back into place. 'If you were a gentleman you wouldn't have touched me at all,' she spat.

'Then perhaps I'm not.' His eyes glittered in the dimness of the tent. 'Perhaps I'm an evil-minded bastard who takes his pleasure at will. Is that what you think, Julie?'

His cruel taunt sent a chill crawling over her skin, made her feel icy-cold despite the warmth of the night. 'I'm quite sure you haven't reached the age you are without pleasuring yourself with a woman or two,' she whispered. 'Were they all willing, or did you force yourself on them as you did me?'

'Force?' There was a grating harshness to his voice. 'Did I use force?'

'Not physically,' she admitted, 'but you used the force of your personality. You must know that you're the sort of man any woman would find attractive. Take Alex, for instance, she's been flirting with you like mad

ever since she arrived—and I've not noticed you reject-
ing her.'

'And that troubles you, does it?'

It was her turn to flash her eyes. 'Hell, no. You're
welcome to her.'

He folded his arms across his magnificent chest. 'It
might interest you to know that I don't want to be
irresistible to all women. I would prefer to be loved by
one woman alone. Do you think that is possible?'

It was a question that surprised Julie, and one she
could not answer. She could not raise her hand and
say, Yes, I think it is possible. I am that woman. I love
you. I will love you forever. He would neither believe
her nor reciprocate her feelings.

'I am waiting for your answer, Julie.'

She swallowed hard. 'Actually, yes, I do.'

'Would *you* marry me, knowing the type of lifestyle
I have?' he asked, his tone brusque.

'Of course I would, if I loved you,' she answered
shakily. She found it practically impossible to hide her
true emotions. 'I'd travel with you to the ends of the
earth. It's no good marrying a man and expecting him
to change. You marry him for the person he is, and if
he's a traveller, an explorer, a scientist—whatever—
then you adapt yourself to his needs. It's as simple as
that.' She put all the depth of her feelings into her
answer—she could not help it. She only hoped he
would not guess that she was speaking from the heart.

'Some man's going to be very lucky,' he said gruffly,
'not many women share your opinion. Will it be Roger,
I wonder? I suspect you've patched things up between
you. I noticed the charming little kiss you gave him
before he left.'

His tone was derogatory and Julie retaliated. 'As a

matter of fact he *has* asked me to go back out with him.'

'I see.' The words were bitter. 'He must love you very much if he's prepared to take you back after the way you treated him.'

'As a further matter of fact,' she retorted, 'he admitted that he had made a——'

But Cameron did not wait to hear what else she had to say. He turned and left her tent as abruptly as he had appeared.

Julie let out a deep breath. It had been a traumatic few minutes. She felt on fire; she still felt Cameron's mouth and hands on her body, still felt excitement running through her veins. Had he been truthful when he'd said he found her irresistible? Or was that a line he used with all girls?

There was no doubt in her mind that he *had* been punishing her, that it *had* been retribution. She had imagined his enjoyment; he had used her, wilfully and forcefully, intent only on destroying her.

The next morning there was nothing on Cameron's face to suggest that there had been any intimacy between them. There was nothing except hard, cold anger, directed at both Ian and herself. After breakfast the two men went off together, the same as they always did, and she was left to her own resources. She once again tried typing, but it hurt too much to lift and use her arm.

Rick and Lee came to talk to her, and it helped pass the time. They knew nothing of her problems. Alex did not even come and ask how her ribs were, remaining down at her own end of the beach, swimming and sunbathing and undoubtedly waiting for Cameron to return.

When the men did finally come back Julie's heart skittered like a mad thing when she caught sight of Cameron, and the depth of her love for him washed over her in painful wave after painful wave.

Ian looked at her tenderly. 'How are you?'

'I'm all right,' she answered.

'Not in too much pain?'

'I'll survive.' It was the pain of unrequited love that hurt most.

'How have you got on with my book?' Cameron barked the question urgently, as though his work was of more importance than her health.

'I haven't done any,' she said quietly. 'I did try but I can't manage it yet; it hurts too much.'

He gave a roar of unexpected anger. 'Am I supposed to believe that? Am I supposed to believe that it's not an excuse to lengthen your remaining time here? Really, Julie, you'll have to try harder than that. Surely your pain is lessening now?'

'No, it isn't,' she insisted. 'Please be patient. I can't help it if I'm not up to it yet.'

'But you could help telling me lies in the first place; how am I to know that you're not lying again?'

And this was what hurt him most of all, she thought unhappily. 'I give you my word,' she said.

Dinner was an uncomfortable, silent occasion, and as soon as Cameron had finished eating he pushed his chair back from the table and disappeared into his tent.

'Has he been like this all day?' asked Julie.

Ian nodded, his lips grim, and there was pain behind his eyes which suggested he was getting one of his migraines. He had been so happy, now everything had crashed about his head; he was utterly, utterly despondent, and Julie wished there was something she could do about it.

When an hour went by and Cameron had still not come out of his tent she walked across to it with sudden determination, saying firmly, 'Cameron, we must talk.'

He lifted his head impatiently from his notebook, eyes cold and distant. 'About what?'

Julie felt her stomach muscles tighten. She had hoped faintly that what she had to say wouldn't be necessary, but it was clear he'd had no change of heart. 'We cannot go on like this.'

His face remained hard and impassive. 'Like what?'

'If you're really finding it too hard to forgive me then I'll go home right now. I want you to radio Jake and tell him to come and fetch me. All I ask is that you give Ian another chance.'

He gave a loud guffaw. 'What makes you think I'd do that? Ian is actually more guilty than you. The masquerade was his idea, wasn't it?'

Julie nodded. 'But I went along with it, so I'm equally to blame. Please, Cameron, be nice to him. Let him stay. This job means so much to him.'

His eyes were contemptuous. 'Such concern is very touching; how I wish I could believe that it's not your own hide you're pleading for. However, my mind is made up; when you go, Ian goes—but not until you have finished my book.'

'Even though I'm not up to it at the moment?'

His lips tightened, as if he was still not sure how genuine she was. 'How long do you think before you'll be fit enough? And I want no thought of malingering,' he added harshly.

'I don't really know,' she answered with a shrug.

'I've never broken my ribs before. A few days, maybe a week.'

'A week?' he echoed. 'That won't do, Julie. It will never be finished in time.'

'I'll make sure it is,' she said quietly, and when he added nothing further she left his tent. He was being totally unreasonable and cold-hearted, she fumed inwardly. He didn't care about her well-being any more, all he was concerned about was getting his damn book finished.

Early the next morning, after an almost sleepless night, Julie heard Alex and Cameron taking what had now become their ritual early-morning swim, the girl shrieking her enjoyment as she and Cameron played games in the water.

Suddenly all went quiet, and Julie's curiosity got the better of her. But when she peeped out of her tent and saw Cameron with his arms around the nubile blonde, kissing her soundly and with obvious enjoyment, she wished she hadn't looked. Raw jealousy began to eat away inside her, so much so that she felt physically sick.

And to make matters worse Cameron announced over breakfast that she need not worry about his book any longer. 'I've just discovered that Alex can type. She is the answer to my prayers. She can take over until you are better.'

Julie felt her heart sink like a lead weight into her stomach. Alex typing out Cameron's book! Alex in their camp, all day and every day! Alex getting closer and closer to Cameron! It was this last thought that bothered her most.

She forced a smile. 'That is good news. I only hope she's good enough.'

A frown moved his thick brows. 'You're not pleased for me? Not aware of the urgency? My publishers have already put the deadline back twice. It has to be finished by the end of the month.'

'I simply know how fussy you are,' she said. 'That's all.'

'And how good you are,' he agreed quietly—surprisingly. 'I told her that if she has any trouble deciphering my writing to ask you.'

'So you're not going to send us home now you've found Alex?' The words were out before she could stop them.

His frown deepened. 'No. Alex is merely stepping into the breach; I don't want to take up too much of her time.'

You won't be doing that, thought Julie bitterly. The girl would enjoy making herself indispensable to him.

And at that very moment Alex came running up to them. 'I'm ready, Cameron,' she said, catching hold of his arm and looking provocatively into the blueness of his eyes. She had a husky, sexy voice at the best of times, but at this moment it was even more sensual, and Julie knew that being ready did not mean sitting typing.

Cameron put his hand over hers and returned her smile warmly. 'Good girl, I'm pleased to see you're so keen. Ian and I are just about to leave but Julie will explain things. She's terribly efficient and has everything under control.'

Alex pouted prettily. 'Won't you be here to show me?' This was obviously what she had expected.

'I'm afraid not.' He pressed a kiss to her brow and then said to Ian, 'Are you ready?'

When he had gone Alex turned petulantly to Julie. 'I suppose I'd better make a start.'

'You suddenly don't sound very happy about it.' Julie looked up at the girl from her chair, knowing full well that Alex had expected Cameron to show her what to do, had thought that the two of them would be spending most of their time together. It was probably the only reason she had offered her services.

Alex lifted her smooth brown shoulders in a carefully controlled gesture. 'Nonsense, I'm delighted I can help. Your accident came at a very bad time for Cameron. The poor man's so concerned about meeting his deadline. It's thrilling, isn't it? I've never worked for an author before. I've never even met one. He's a most fascinating man.'

Her eyes sparkled as she spoke and Julie began to feel the green-eyed monster eating away inside her again. This girl was hiding nothing; she was intent on a holiday romance with Cameron and didn't care who saw it. She had no inkling that Julie was in love with him because, as far as she was aware, Julie was safely married to Ian.

After showing Alex the set-up, explaining what needed to be done and how each page was to be set out, Julie left her to it. She sat with a magazine on her lap, out of sight, but able to hear clearly the tap of the typewriter keys, the exclamations of anger when the girl went wrong, the tearing of sheets of paper from the machine and the fresh ones being inserted.

It wasn't as convenient as using a word processor, when mistakes could be corrected on the screen before printing, and the fact that it was a very old portable as well didn't help. It was necessary to bang down on the keys instead of just touching them, and this was one of the reasons why Julie had trouble; each pressure of her fingers sent a pain shooting through her side.

After a while the sound of typing finished and Alex emerged from beneath the office awning, flexing her shoulders and her fingers and looking not a little disgruntled. 'Where did he get that typewriter from? The Ark? Lord, I'm exhausted already, and I've only done three pages.'

'It takes a bit of getting used to,' Julie agreed, wondering if the girl was wishing she had not agreed to do it, but not daring to ask.

'Will Cameron be back soon?'

Julie shook her head. 'They always take a packed lunch.'

Alex pouted. 'I hope he doesn't expect me to work all day and every day. I didn't know it would be like this. It's far too tiring, especially in this heat. I'm going for a swim.'

It was almost four before the blonde returned for another typing session and even then she only lasted an hour. Julie said nothing, but it secretly pleased her that Alex wasn't coping as well as Cameron had hoped.

She got up and began preparations for their evening meal—scrubbing sweet potatoes, ready to boil in their jackets, opening a tin of sausages and baked beans to go with them. It was basic food but nourishing and satisfying, and they always seemed to enjoy whatever she did.

Alex had changed back into her bikini again and was bathing in the stretch of water right in front of their camp. It was taking a liberty, thought Julie, and she was making it very obvious that she was waiting for

Cameron to come back and join her. Which was exactly what he did.

He always took a swim on his return, but Julie had thought he would at least come and find out how Alex had got on. It appeared he wanted to ask her in person.

'What's wrong?' asked Ian, when he saw her face.

Julie's eyes shot daggers in Alex's direction. 'Do I have to tell you? She's flirted with him like mad ever since they got here.'

Ian frowned. 'I hadn't noticed.'

'Men!' she exclaimed through gritted teeth.

'I'm sorry, Sis,' He put his arm around her. 'But I'm sure nothing will come of it. She's not his type.'

'How do you know who is his type?' she asked furiously.

'She's too young.'

'And very beautiful.'

'He'll never fall for her.'

'Would you?'

'I love Julie.'

'Dammit,' she cried, 'I mean if you weren't married, if you weren't in love with someone else.'

He considered her question. 'No, I don't think so. Men prefer to do the chasing. As a matter of fact, I think I'll join them. Are you coming?'

'I'm not up to it,' she said, 'but you go ahead.' And although it wasn't in Julie's nature to be spiteful she felt pleased when she saw Alex's scowl of annoyance, and even more so when the girl left the water to rejoin her cousins.

Over dinner Cameron did finally ask her how Alex had got on.

'I believe she's finding it hard going,' answered Julie. 'Mmm, she did say something about finding the typewriter a mean machine. I wasn't sure what she meant. I've never had any trouble with it myself.'

'That's because men tend to pound the keys,' she pointed out. 'Have you ever used a computer?'

'Frequently.'

'Then you must know the difference.'

'I didn't hear *you* complain.'

She shrugged. 'What was the point?'

And, apart from asking her how her ribs were, that was the extent of their conversation. He retired to write out his day's notes, Ian too, and Julie went to bed. But she did not get undressed, she was wide awake and knew she wouldn't sleep for hours. Maybe she would take a walk later, when all was quiet, when the others had settled down for the night and when she could be alone with her thoughts and her yearnings.

It was almost eleven before she finally emerged from her tent and strolled down to the water's edge. Everywhere was in darkness; everyone was safely sleeping. A Galapagos owl laughed, the weird cackling noise startling her.

She walked to the lagoon and back, and was about to re-enter her tent when she heard the sound of muted voices. She frowned and listened. They appeared to be coming from Cameron's tent, and a few minutes later a dark shape came out and ran lightly along the beach to the other end.

Julie felt like screaming. She felt like chasing after Alex and telling her to leave Cameron alone, and she crawled back into her tent, knowing there would be no sleep for her now tonight—or any night while their visitors remained.

# CHAPTER TEN

AFTER a few days spent typing out Cameron's book, Alex began to show signs of unrest. She started work much later each morning, taking a three-hour break during the hottest part of the day and finishing long before the men came back. It was only in Cameron's company that she became alive, and he had no idea of the tantrums she threw in his absence. Indeed, he still showed a definite interest in the girl, much to Julie's distress.

Julie never said anything to Cameron about the girl's work, although he could not have failed to notice that his book was not progessing as quickly as he had hoped.

And then one morning Alex announced to Julie that she was going off with her cousins for the whole day.

'Does Cameron know?' she asked.

Alex shrugged. 'No, but I'm sure he won't mind.' She looked supremely confident, as though she could do anything and get away with it. 'We might even go and find him, see what sort of work it is that takes him away for such long hours at a time.'

'I'm not sure that he'd like being interrupted,' said Julie.

'Maybe he wouldn't like it if *you* dared do such a thing,' returned Alex. 'You work here, you're employed by him; there is a difference. I'm sure he won't mind stopping to talk to *me*.' And she skipped away down the beach.

Julie reluctantly decided that it was probably true, and the thought niggled at her. She sat brooding for ages before finally wading out into the ocean for her daily dip. She was unable to use the lagoon yet because of the exertion needed to haul herself out.

When Cameron unexpectedly appeared at her side Julie got the fright of her life. For once she had not sensed his presence, had not experienced the tingle of awareness he usually caused. The shock of seeing him made her gasp, and as she turned to face him she somehow lost her footing.

As she was in only a few inches of water Julie had visions of giving her broken ribs a nasty jolt as she hit the coral. But strong arms saved her, and the brief spasm of pain seemed of no consequence compared to the turbulent sensations Cameron's touch evoked— made all the more intense because she was naked!

Thinking she would be alone for the whole day, Julie had decided she could get away without wearing her swimsuit; now her trembling body was held against Cameron's bare chest, and the sudden contact seemed to have a disturbing effect on him too. His eyes darkened as they stood there together, and he made no attempt to let her go. Julie could actually feel the sudden unremitting thud of his heart, as well as her own, racing in desperate response.

'You shouldn't be out here,' he muttered thickly.

'I need to bathe.' At least he still had his shorts on.

'Not by yourself,' he growled. 'Not in your condition.'

She wished he would let her go, and fear that she could unwittingly give herself away made her say sharply, 'I was under the impression you thought I was putting it on.'

'Maybe I did say that in the heat of the moment,' he agreed off-handedly. 'I was worried about my book. I still am, as a matter of fact, Alex isn't proving as good a typist as I'd hoped. Where is she, by the way? I came to discuss some alterations and found the camp deserted.'

'She's gone off for the day with Rick and Lee,' answered Julie, hating herself for feeling pleased that the girl had been caught out.

'I guess she deserves some time off,' he said surprisingly. 'It is her holiday, after all.'

Julie felt an unreasoning spasm of anger that he could be so understanding where Alex was concerned and yet so damning in her own case. 'Let me go, Cameron,' she said, her voice filled with pain.

'I'm hurting you, I'm sorry.' He relaxed his hold on her slightly but not altogether, and his vivid blue eyes looked into hers. Then with a groan he said, 'Damn you, woman, you're as tempting as ever.'

His mouth found hers before she could do anything about it; and out there in the ocean they stood together and kissed. It was something Julie had never thought would happen again, and although she knew it meant nothing to him, that it was pure physical hunger that drove him, she could not find it in her to protest.

Her hunger equalled his; her need was as strong— stronger—her desire as intense. Without thought for the consequences, forgetting everything except that she was being held in the arms of the man she loved, she returned his kiss, parting her lips, letting his tongue entwine with hers, feeling her breasts harden and thrust against the hard muscular wall of his chest. It was like drinking sweet nectar itself.

It was not until Cameron's kiss deepened, until she

felt his surge of desire and the compulsive tightening of his arms, the groan in the back of his throat, the thrusting of his hips, that sanity began to surface. It was all very well letting him kiss her, her conscience would let her live with that, but if it went any further then she would never forgive herself.

Her mind started to scream her resistance and she attempted to push him away, ignoring the pain, intent only on freeing herself from the raw danger Cameron now posed.

He tensed for an instant, seeming taken by surprise by her sudden change of mood, and then his kiss began again with renewed urgency.

'No, Cameron. No!' she gritted against his teeth. 'I won't let you.'

'You want this as much as me,' he rasped harshly.

'No, I don't. I don't.'

Somehow—perhaps because her body was still wet, perhaps from sheer desperation—she managed to slip down out of the circle of his arms, but in so doing she again lost her balance and went sprawling ignominiously into the water. The jarring effect was every bit as intense as she had feared and she lay a moment, waiting for the pain to subside.

This time Cameron did not rescue her; instead, before she had regained her breath, he joined her, his arms pinning her to the coarse, gritty coral, not hurting, but allowing her no movement either.

She stared up at him, her eyes wide with shock, unable to speak, unable to believe that he was taking advantage like this. His blue eyes were glazed, his breathing ragged, his skin flushed, and there was an expression on his face which told her all too clearly that he had every intention of assuaging his hunger.

Julie's hair floated and drifted in a dark cloud in the water, framing her face attractively. She had no idea how hauntingly beautiful she looked, the sea-water cushioning her, lapping around her ears, virtually into her mouth, giving her an almost ethereal image.

Cameron could not stop looking at her, eyes devouring, raw hunger on his handsome face, which inched in slow motion towards her. She could not move. Even had it not been for the constriction of his arms she would have been unable to do so. She was transfixed, totally numbed, and her eyes were on his mouth, captivated, fascinated, her own lips parting in response as his took hers with an urgency that shot painful, tingling sensation through every vein and artery in her body.

His hands began to move over her, tracing the outline of her slender legs, her thighs, moving over the flatness of her stomach, creeping with tantalising slowness to the aching fullness of her breasts.

She gave a tiny gasp of pleasure when his hands finally captured her, his fingers seeking her hardened but sensitive nipples. It was sweet, sweet torture, incredibly erotic, as the ocean washed over them with the gentle ebb and flow of the tide.

His mouth was bruising in its intensity but Julie had no thought now to pull away; her capitulation was complete. She loved this man with every fibre of her being, and if this was the only way she could experience such torturous pleasure then so be it. It was better than nothing. It was a memory she could rekindle at a later date and savour to the full. No one would be able to take it away.

Freely and hungrily she gave herself to him; wantonly her body moved in urgent rhythm, the buoyancy of the ocean making movements easier and virtually pain-free. She had lost all inhibitions, was oblivious now to her nudity. She knew only that she wanted this man with a primitive hunger that had never assailed her before.

It was like being in another world, a world of sensations that transcended earthly feelings. It was like being in paradise, and she could imagine just the two of them here on this island—alone—forever.

'Julie,' he muttered thickly against her mouth. 'Oh, Julie, what are you doing to me?'

There was no answer she could make. Her response was a whimper in the back of her throat, another thrust of her body against his, and his hands on her tightened. Dear lord, how she loved him. Best not to remember that this meant nothing to him, that he was pleasuring himself alone, with no thought at all for her own feelings.

Except that she was showing no signs of resistance! She was as bad as he, urging their bodies together, her tongue exploring his mouth, nibbling his lips as he did hers, following his lead in absolutely everything he did.

She had never felt such complete abandonment; had indeed never let anyone get this close, not even Roger. It was as if she were being propelled by outside forces, forces stronger than life itself. It was as if her whole body had been taken over and she had no say in anything it felt or did.

Only the tips of her breasts protruded above the sea-water, and when he took each of them in turn into his mouth her agony of longing increased. She moulded his head in her palms, writhing beneath him, wanting more, needing more, knowing there was nothing he could not do to her in her present aroused state.

And when his hands moved down her body, to explore again the flatness of her stomach, the curve of her hips and the softness of her thighs, she gave a moan of sheer pleasure, her head arching back into the water, her throat exposed, her body lifted, unconsciously offering herself to him.

He kissed her mouth again and she could taste the salt-water on his lips, could smell the tantalising maleness of him. He filled her nostrils; he filled her with desire that was almost out of control.

Then he cupped her face and looked deep into her eyes, and there was a sudden wretchedness in him that she could not understand. 'Damn you, Julie,' he grated. 'You're a siren and a temptress. The ring you wore temporarily protected you, but now——' he suddenly wrenched the slim gold band from her finger and threw it far out into the ocean '—there is nothing to save you from me.'

'There is Alex,' she reminded him huskily, feeling suddenly fearful.

'Alex?' He looked surprised and then amused. 'Yes, of course. Alex—beautiful, sexy Alex.' And then his face hardened. 'There is also Roger,' he slammed. 'But they're not here, are they? There is just you and me and these feelings that neither of us can do anything about.'

Did that mean——? No, it couldn't—could it? Julie looked at him with wide, troubled eyes. 'What are you—saying?'

'That I'm going to make love to you, woman,' he grated. 'Right here and now, and don't try to fight me because it's as clear as the nose on your beautiful face that you want this as much as me.'

Julie closed her eyes, needing to shut out his savage

mastery. She could not bear to look at him, could not bear to give way to the agony of knowing he was right, so very, very right.

'Look at me, damn you,' he muttered, his fingers hard on her chin.

She swallowed hard and reluctantly dragged open heavy lids. They looked at each other for many long, testing moments, hearts throbbing in unison, bodies trembling. Julie knew she had only to make one move for him to carry out his threat, one tiny sound of acquiescence. She could not do it; she could not shoulder the responsibility for such a momentous decision.

All of a sudden he gave a heavy, pained growl. 'Your ribs, dammit; I'd forgotten your ribs.' But he did not move away, he continued to touch and stroke and incite, though his actions were gentler now.

It was a most incredibly erotic experience, and it took all of Julie's willpower not to touch him as he was touching her. It was temptation beyond compare and how she managed to control herself she did not know.

'Because of your damned pretence,' he muttered, stroking the tip of her nose, 'I've been forced to keep my desires in check. I didn't want to give the impression that I was lusting over a married woman, but believe me——'

Lusting! The word repeated itself over and over in Julie's mind, and she heard no more of what he said. Lusting, lust, fleshly desire, lasciviousness. That was all it was. The words torched her brain.

He was using her. He had no morals, he was merely satisfying his own carnal cravings. She had chosen to ignore it because of her own selfish needs, and now it was destroying her.

The more Julie thought about it, the more angry she got. 'Stop that, Cameron. Get away. You have no right doing this to me.' Her hazel eyes, more green than brown at this moment, sparked her hostility.

Surprised by her sudden attack, Cameron frowned. 'Aren't you a bit late in protesting?'

'How could I fight you with this?' she snapped, putting her hand to her ribs. 'You certainly pick your moments.'

She scrambled to her feet and he gave her a hand, but he let her go once they were standing. 'You're suggesting I took advantage because you could put up no resistence?' There was the darkness of thunder-clouds on his brow.

'Didn't you?'

'No, I damn well did not,' he grated, 'and you know it. Neither of us were able to help ourselves. It was inevitable.'

Julie frowned faintly. 'Inevitable? I don't really think that——'

'Dammit,' he cut in angrily, 'can you deny that the day I picked you up there was a spark of something between us?'

Julie felt a quiver run through the very core of her, but her eyes flashed. 'Oh, yes, there was a spark all right. A spark of anger, a spark of hostility. You were annoyed because you'd had to come and fetch me, and I was furious because I'd been kept waiting in the atrocious heat without so much as a hat to protect my head.'

His narrowed eyes rested on her face for several long seconds. 'Maybe I was a litle annoyed at having to take time out of my busy schedule, but, hell, Julie, you more than made up for it. Not quite dressed for the situation,' he added with a wry smile, 'but that was part of your charm. You were beautifully indignant.'

'And you were hateful,' she protested.

'You didn't like me just a teeny little bit?'

'No.'

'I think you're lying. I think you felt the same. I think you were totally frustrated because of your *pretence*.' He spat the word, angry for a moment.

Julie shook her head in disbelief. 'How could I have been attracted when I was just getting over my affair with Roger? I didn't want another man in my life.'

'How about the poor guy you saw behind Roger's back?' he sneered. 'Why don't you admit it, Julie? You're a very sensual woman. You're no actress—you could never put on such pleasure, such aching need; it has to be a part of you. You are as guilty as I am, and I can assure you that there will come a time when neither of us will be able to stop ourselves.'

Julie stared at him speechlessly, seeing the glitter of blue through narrowed lids. How dared he say such things? How dared he assume she was like this with every man she met? He clearly thought he only had to touch her, to look at her in a certain way, to have her melt in his arms, to give in to his every whim, to give her body willingly to his.

It was true, but she would never let him see it. Fierce determination took the place of surprise. 'You're mistaken. I'm not like that at all. And don't think I'll ever let you touch me again. I find your behaviour totally inexcusable, especially considering your relationship with Alex.'

'My—*relationship* with Alex?' Again he looked amused. 'And, pray, what is that supposed to be?'

'As if you didn't know,' she snapped. 'You're a bastard, Cameron Storm, and I hate you.'

'You know what they say hate's akin to?' Still his mouth twitched.

'I wouldn't fall in love with you if were the last man on earth,' she cried in panic. 'You're a lecherous beast without any thought at all for people's feelings.'

'Is that what you think?' A frown carved his brow, drew black brows together, darkened his eyes. Even a muscle jerked in his jaw; she had clearly hit a raw spot.

And she was glad. Glad, glad, glad. She wanted to hurt him. He was hurting her, so why shouldn't she turn the tables? 'It's the picture I'm getting. Is it me or Alex you're really interested in? Or neither of us? You're just playing with us because we happen to be available. You're never going to get married but you're going to have fun along the way, and you don't care if you break any hearts.'

At last he thrust her from him, his eyes hard and judgemental. 'If that is your opinion then maybe we're two of a kind. Maybe we suit each other much better than you think.'

'You swine! You started all of this,' she declared in outrage as she headed back towards their camp.

'But you made no attempt to stop me.' He fell in beside her.

'I couldn't.'

'Or didn't want to,' he responded, with a mocking curl to his lips.

'I hate you.' She snatched up a baggy T-shirt from the chair where she had left it and pulled it over her head. It came halfway down her thighs and she felt safe at last—except from her own thoughts.

'You have a beautiful body, Julie.'

She felt her cheeks flame.

'Roger's a lucky guy.'

She could have told him then that she had turned Roger down, but she didn't. She needed a buffer, someone to keep Cameron at arm's length. She wasn't strong enough to do it herself.

'Tell me, are you as inhibited with Roger as you were with me? Has he sampled the delights of your delectable body? Has he inhaled the sweet, heady scent of you until it drives him crazy?'

Horrified by what he was saying, Julie looked into the intent blueness of his eyes and saw the dangerous gleam. 'You have no right speaking to me like that.'

Dark brows rose. 'Has no man ever said such things to you before? Hasn't Roger told you what a sensation you are?'

'You're disgusting!' she cried.

'And you're beautiful. Shall I fix us some lunch?'

Julie was glad he had changed the subject, but she would really have liked to spend some time on her own; she needed to regain the equilibrium he had shot to pieces.

'Where are your sandwiches?' she asked ungraciously.

'I left them behind.'

'Then oughtn't you to be getting back? Won't Ian wonder where you are?'

His lips curved. 'Are you trying to get rid of me, Julie?'

She saw no point in lying. 'As a matter of fact, yes.'

'Then I'm afraid you're going to be disappointed. I've decided to stay here for the rest of the day. Why don't you sit in the shade while I make us a meal?'

Julie was not in the least hungry. She was far too

confused and disturbed by the morning's events to entertain the idea of food, but at least with him in the kitchen it would give her a few minutes' respite.

She deliberately sat where she could not see Cameron, otherwise she knew her eyes would constantly stray in his direction. They would be drawn to him like a magnet, giving away her inner torment, telling him all too clearly that she had been lying when she'd said there was no attraction.

Her body actually still tingled in the aftermath of his lovemaking, and the hunger in her had increased a thousandfold. She knew without a doubt that when she finally returned to England she would be as unhappy as Ian had been when his wife left him. 'Unhappy' wasn't even a strong enough word; she would be desolate, totally destroyed.

It suddenly occurred to her, thinking about her twin, that she was being entirely selfish for the first time in her life. She ought to be thinking more about Ian, not herself. His was a double calamity—first the loss of Julie, now the loss of the job that had been helping to restore his peace of mind.

She would get over Cameron eventually, far more quickly than Ian would get over this second set-back. It was a fact of life that time healed all wounds. Ian had been married to his Julie for eighteen months; they had bonded together, had shared their love, and it was obvious that he had been hurt far more than she was now.

Her love was new—a few days old—and very private. It belonged to herself alone. There were few memories to dwell over. She and Cameron had had nothing— nothing except a few kisses. She would be a fool to grieve over something she had never had.

'Lunch is ready.' Cameron's cheerful voice broke into her thoughts. 'Come and get it.'

Julie pushed herself painfully up out of her chair and crossed to the fold-up table they always used at meal-times, feeling her heart lurch all over again as she caught sight of him.

He had pulled on a shirt, but it hid none of his ravaging power. His eyes were brooding, despite his light-hearted tone, and she wondered whether he was as disturbed as she by the morning's events, or whether he was planning his next invasion of her privacy. It was a daunting thought.

They had used up all their fresh supplies and were living out of tins and packets now, supplemented occasionally by lobster or *langostas* caught by Cameron. There were fish in abundance outside the bay, but the currents were too dangerous for any of them to venture that far, and there were no fruit trees of any kind on the island, so their diet was becoming a bit monotonous.

For the first time in her life Julie had made bread, and although it never seemed to turn out the same twice neither of the men ever complained. She had been expecting a sandwich now, either ham or corned beef on the stodgy bread, but instead Cameron had opened tins of salmon, potatoes and peas.

He had also opened a bottle of wine that had been sitting in the refrigerator since they arrived, pouring her a glass now with great ceremony. It was almost as though he was turning today into a celebration, thought Julie worriedly.

He held up his glass. 'To us.'

Us? she questioned silently. She could not join him in such a toast, not in the present circumstances. 'I think to your book, instead,' she said. 'I wish you every success with it.'

His lips quirked his disapproval as he followed her lead. 'To my book, then—if it is ever typed out in time.' And some of the *bonhomie* had gone out of his voice.

'Of course it will be,' she said. 'I won't be this way forever.'

'It's taking you long enough,' he growled. 'And Alex is pitifully slow. Would there, by any chance, still be some thoughts going through your beautiful head that I might, given time, change my mind about letting you and Ian stay? Is that what the procrastination is all about?'

Julie closed her eyes, devastated that he was speaking like this after all that had happened earlier. Did he, despite everything, really think she was capable of such devious behaviour?

'What's wrong?' he jeered. 'Have I touched a nerve? Have I hit on the truth?'

His harsh tone grated over raw nerve-endings and Julie shot him a look of pure hatred. 'I doubt you'd believe me if I denied it.'

'I think I have just cause to be suspicious.'

'Really?' she flashed.

'Really. I come back unexpectedly and what do I see? Not you nursing your wounds, but you taking a swim in the sea, enjoying your new-found leisure.'

'You swine!' Julie flared. 'I was not swimming, as you well know, I was merely paddling, I was trying to wash myself.'

'So you say.'

'It is the truth,' she gritted.

'We'll never prove otherwise, will we?' he taunted.

'Eat your food before the mocking-birds get it.' Already the fearless birds were stalking the edge of the table, eyes cocked on the food on their plates.

'They can have it; I don't want it,' cried Julie with unusual rancour, and with one swift, furious movement of her arm she swept the whole lot on to the floor.

She regretted it a second later, felt appalled by her childish behaviour. It had been a silly thing to do and totally unlike her, and the circumstances certainly had not warranted such a deed. But she could not step down; it would be too degrading by far. He shouldn't have taunted her. He shouldn't have made offensive accusations that hadn't an ounce of truth in them.

Expecting Cameron to be angry at her action, Julie was astonished when he roared with hearty laughter. 'What a refreshing change you are, Julie Drummond. My time spent here is usually with equally serious scientists. No one ever does anything outrageous.'

Unable to stop herself, Julie joined in his laughter, feeling once again the spark igniting between them, feeling a resurgence of her senses, feeling herself gravitating towards him. Until suddenly Alex came running across the beach towards them.

## CHAPTER ELEVEN

ALEX looked from Cameron to Julie and back again to Cameron, and then down to the remnants of the meal on the floor, and there was something in her eyes that Julie could not quite fathom. 'So here you are, Cameron,' she said, keeping her tone light, though Julie could see the effort it cost her. 'I've been looking for you.'

'And I came back to look for you.' He made it sound very special, as though he had been seeking her out for reasons other than to do with his book.

Jealousy stirred viciously within Julie's stomach and she wished herself a thousand miles away. It was unreal that he could speak to Alex like this when minutes earlier he had been making love to her.

Obviously Cameron thought, through whatever garbled version of the story Roger had told him, that she, Julie, was easy prey for any man, that she welcomed their advances, even. And by not fighting him off she had confirmed it. He would use her, but he would never get serious about her. And, if the truth were known, it was probably still retribution he sought. Alex was a different kettle of fish altogether.

'Will you excuse us, Julie?' he said, taking Alex's elbow as he led her towards the 'office'.

Violent emotion twisted Julie's nerves and she got to her feet, wishing there was somewhere she could escape to. The beach suddenly felt like a prison. The only way out was up the cliffs, but as that was an impossibility she walked to the lagoon instead. It wasn't far enough to put any real distance between them; Alex's peals of laughter reached her and she felt as though a lead weight had settled in the bottom of her stomach.

Eventually, her thoughts still too turbulent for comfort, she made her way back. Cameron was nowhere in sight and Alex, surprisingly, was at the desk typing. He had obviously *persuaded* her—no doubt with an excess of tender kisses, thought Julie bitterly—to carry on with his book.

As Julie approached the girl looked up, and her face was astonishingly contorted with fury; indeed, she looked quite ugly, an amazing transformation from her normal stunning good looks. 'What's going on between you and Cameron?'

Julie lifted her brows in surprise. 'What makes you think there is anything going on?'

Alex pushed herself to her feet and came to stand only inches from her. 'Don't come the innocent. I saw you in the water from the cliff-top. I saw him kissing you—I saw you kissing him.'

Julie felt mortified, more so because she had been wearing nothing but her birthday suit! But she showed none of her distress, instead her chin lifted and she smiled. 'I guess all's fair in love and war.'

'You bitch!' snapped Alex. 'I'm going to tell Ian what you're up to, and he won't be very happy when he finds out that his wife is two-timing him.'

'Ian's not my husband.' Julie told her calmly.

'What?' screeched the blonde, frowning ferociously.

'I said, Ian is not my husband.' Julie quite enjoyed the other girl's distress.

'Then what——?'

'He's my brother—my twin brother. We were—playing a game.'

'Cameron knows?'

'Of course he does.'

'Is that what all the shouting was about the other day when you had your visitor? Is that when he found out?'

Julie inclined her head. 'As a matter of fact, yes, but he wasn't angry for long. All is now forgiven and forgotten.'

Alex frowned. 'I don't understand.'

'It's a long story,' said Julie. 'I'm sure you wouldn't be interested.'

'And now you're making a play for Cameron, is that it?' demanded Alex.

Julie smiled. 'Actually, it's the other way round.'

The blonde swore disbelievingly. 'You're a liar. It's you who's chasing him.'

Julie continued to smile, even though her heart felt like lead. 'The same as you are? It should be fun, shouldn't it? I wonder which one of us will get our man?'

Alex's eyes flashed. 'I don't think there's any doubt about it.' And she swung around and resumed her seat at the desk, attacking the typewriter with unnecessary vigour.

Julie found herself some shade behind her tent. The confrontation, coming on top of everything else, had been thoroughly unsettling. She was convinced that Cameron had unashamedly taken advantage of her this morning. Her only consolation, the only salve to her wounded pride, was the fact that he thought she was like this with every man. At least he hadn't guessed that she was in love with him. That would have been the final humiliation.

She closed her eyes and must have dozed, because she suddenly heard Alex talking, and it wasn't to Cameron, nor was it to Rick or Lee. It sounded suspiciously like Roger, but how could that be? Was she dreaming?

She got up and there he was, deep in conversation with Alex. Julie felt utterly confused. The whole thing was turning into a farce. Instead of the three of them spending time here quietly by themselves they were being invaded by people who posed all sorts of problems.

'Roger?' She approached him from behind.

He turned and gave her a warm, yet faintly guilty smile.

'What are you doing back here so soon?'

'To see how you are faring, of course, my darling, before I go back to England.' He gave her a kiss on the brow and held her carefully. 'How are your ribs?'

'Mending, I hope.' She caught sight of Alex's puzzled face. This really would give the girl something to think about.

' I thought I might stay a day or two,' said Roger. 'Do you think Cameron will mind?'

Julie shrugged. 'You know him better than me.'

'I've brought my tent. I think I'll pitch it in any case. What time will they be back?'

'When they're hungry,' returned Julie, and she glanced at her watch, amazed to see how much time had gone by. 'Actually, that shouldn't be too long.'

Out of the corner of her eye she saw Alex still looking at them curiously, and she wondered how much, if anything, Roger had told her. She hoped nothing. She would prefer to keep their private life private.

She opened a couple of tins of chicken in wine and put some rice on to boil, and waited with trepidation for her brother and Cameron to return. By turning up again like this Roger would confirm Cameron's belief that they had patched up their differences, and, although Roger could be the protection she needed, it left Alex a clear field.

This was what bothered her most. Up until today, she had never been sure how serious the girl was—whether it came naturally to her to be a tease. It seemed that now she knew Julie could be an adversary she would go all out to win Cameron's affection.

Cameron's face, when he did return, was a picture of conflicting emotions—politeness forcing him to welcome his friend, suspicion that he was here for Julie's sake, and anger that they were being invaded once again.

'I thought I'd stay a night or two before I head home,' said Roger. 'I hope you don't mind?'

'Would it make any difference if I did?' barked Cameron, looking condemningly at Julie as he spoke.

Roger appeared a little taken aback by this vehemence. 'I'm sorry, I didn't realise it would cause so much inconvenience.'

'It's all right.' Cameron shook his head in self-anger. 'I've had a hell of a day. You've caught me at a bad time, that's all.'

A hell of a day! Was that how he saw it? thought Julie bitterly. He had virtually made love to her and it had been hell! She felt totally demoralised all of a sudden. Thank goodness Alex was no longer around to hear him say this or she would never-endingly crow her delight.

The three men went for a swim while she laid the

table, and Alex, for once, was conspicuous by her absence, though Julie saw her down at the other end of the beach, constantly looking in their direction.

Much to Julie's dismay, Roger gave her his undivided attention during the meal. Cameron continued to scowl, and Ian seemed to be wondering what was going on. But Julie knew she would never tell her twin about Cameron's attempts to make love to her—and her own unmitigated response!

After supper Cameron disappeared into his tent. Roger produced a pack of cards and the three of them played rummy until Ian declared that he was going to bed. By this time Julie was tired too, but Roger put his hand on hers when she made to get up.

'What's wrong with Cameron?' he asked in a hushed voice. 'I've never seen him like this before.'

Julie grimaced. 'Then you're lucky.'

'But it's unlike him,' insisted Roger. 'He's always calm and unruffled, and the sanest person I know. Something's gone wrong, that's for sure. He's still not mad at you and Ian for lying?'

'Some,' she admitted.

'No! He can't be. It's out of all proportion. It's ridiculous. Is it bothering you? Would you like me to have a word with him?'

Julie held up her hands in horror. 'Please, don't say a word. You'll only make matters worse. He'll get over it—eventually.' It was best that Roger thought it was this at the root of Cameron's anger.

She was undressed and in bed, reliving again Cameron's kisses, still feeling his caresses, when she heard movements outside her tent. She gave a faint cry of alarm when Cameron's body blocked the opening. She knew it was him this time; he was the only one who ever dared invade her privacy. 'What do you want?' she whispered fiercely.

He came in and hunkered down at the side of her bed. 'I want to know what Roger's doing here,' he growled, his voice still tight with anger.

'He wanted to say goodbye,' she replied defensively, 'and to see how my ribs are doing.'

'And you invited him to stay?' asked Cameron, his voice filled with derision.

'No!' she said at once. 'That was his own idea.'

'Hmph!' he growled. 'It's very clear that now you've made it up he can't keep away from you. He's more of a fool than I thought. Any woman who gives her body to another man as easily as you do isn't worth wasting time on.'

Julie said nothing. What could she say? She had let Cameron believe she and Roger had made it up. To change her story now would do no good. He would think she was lying—yet again.

'Have you nothing to say in your own defence?' he rasped.

Julie shook her head.

'I cannot hear you.'

'No,' she whispered achingly.

'Damn you, woman.' He knelt over her and took her face between his palms, and she could see the faint glittering light in his eyes. She thought he was going to kiss her, and knew that if he did she wouldn't be able to do a thing about it.

'It was the worst thing I ever did, suggesting Ian bring his wife.'

'For me too,' she whispered passionately. 'Do you think I'm enjoying this? Do you think I enjoy being the butt of your anger?'

'I think you enjoy me making love to you,' he muttered harshly. 'I can sense your response even now; I can feel your excitement.'

'No, you can't,' cried Julie in panic, trying to thrash her head from side to side, desperately trying to escape his vice-like grip. 'No!'

'Then what is it you feel?' he questioned fiercely.

'Anger!' she told him strongly. 'Disgust that you dare try to take advantage of your so-called friend's girl. Some friend you are proving to be.'

'*Try* to take advantage?' he asked with a cynical smile. '*Try*?' Eyebrows rose mockingly. 'You were one very willing participant, Julie. Deny it if you dare.'

'You're not an easy man to resist when you set out to charm,' she protested. 'Do I have to tell you that yet again? I lay the blame in your court. You shouldn't have started anything when you knew I was back with Roger.'

'Are you saying you are so weak-willed that you let any man take you who tries?' His eyes were suddenly savage again.

'I am saying nothing of the kind,' she returned defensively, realising, sickeningly, that she had said the wrong thing. 'And I demand that you get out of this tent right now, before I shout for Roger. Would you like him to see what sort of a man you really are?'

Eyes glinted dangerously. 'How you love to turn the tables. I think Roger would be more interested in hearing that you haven't reformed after all.'

Julie lay limply against the pillows, all the fight knocked out of her. He could be very cruel, this man, devastatingly so.

'You're giving up the battle, are you?' he derided. 'You've suddenly decided that you can't win?'

'Just get out,' she said wearily.

'I think maybe I'll take another kiss first.'

Her eyes flashed. 'You swine!'

'You're so beautifully angry.'

'I hate you.'

'And, despite your being all I despise in a woman, I still can't resist you.' His head swooped, and Julie was unable to avoid him.

# CHAPTER TWELVE

CAMERON'S kiss was punishing, intent only on humiliation, bruising Julie's lips, determined to draw out a
response, grinding her lips back against her teeth until
she felt the salt taste of her own blood.

She fought her feelings, fought the quagmire of
emotions that surfaced, remained resolutely limp until
finally, with harsh, derogatory laughter, as if he knew
of her inner struggle, he let her go and disappeared
from the tent.

Julie knew she ought to be disgusted and furious by
his behaviour but she wasn't. Although his kiss had
been meant to hurt and punish, she had experienced
nothing but pleasure and excitement. It seemed as
though love had biased her mind where this man was
concerned. She could only hope and pray that there
would be no further repeat, because it would be
impossible to deny him yet again.

It took her a long while to get to sleep.

She was woken at dawn by Alex's excited voice. Again
she was out swimming with Cameron. But then Julie
heard Roger as well, and could not resist peeping out
of her tent to see how Alex was taking it. Poor Roger,
he wouldn't know that he was being an unwanted third
party. He had no idea that Alex had set her sights on
Cameron.

The girl was scowling but she continued to swim, and
when the three of them came out of the water she took

Cameron's hand and stood on tiptoe to kiss him. It was a light kiss that could have meant nothing or everything. Julie was certainly not fooled.

Roger looked surprised and left them to it, and he said to Julie later, when she was preparing breakfast, 'I didn't realise Alex and Cameron were—an item.' It seemed to disturb him.

'It's nothing serious,' she answered. At least, that was what she kept telling herself.

'Cameron's a sworn bachelor.'

'I know, he told me.'

'How much longer is she likely to remain?'

Julie shrugged. 'I guess until I'm fit enough to take over. I suppose I ought to try, though it still hurts like hell when I move.'

'Cameron's lucky he's found someone else to do his work, don't you think?'

'Maybe.' And there was something in her voice that made Roger look at her sharply.

'What's wrong? Don't you like Alex?'

'It's not that,' she said quickly. 'She's not really very good. I don't know why Cameron puts up with her.'

Roger grinned. 'Probably because she has a fantastic body.' And then he pulled a face. 'I'm sorry, that wasn't meant to be disrespectful—you're in pretty good shape yourself.' And as if to make up he leaned across the table and kissed her.

After breakfast Cameron invited Roger to join him and Ian. 'Otherwise you're going to be bored out of your mind.'

'With two beautiful women to keep me company?' queried Roger mockingly.

'I don't want you to disturb Alex,' announced

Cameron sternly, 'and Julie is still not up to par. She needs to rest.'

'I wouldn't dream of putting any pressure on either of them,' said Roger. 'But I will stay here, if you don't mind.'

It was clear Cameron did mind, and Julie could not understand why. Why shouldn't Roger spend time with her? Why should he spend the whole day studying fur seals? Roger's interest in ecology was nowhere near as intent as Cameron's or Ian's. It was a hobby with him, that was all.

And so her brother and Cameron left, and after she had tidied the kitchen she and Roger sat and put the world to rights. Their conversation was desultory, and occasionally he wandered over to where Alex sat typing to ask whether he could get her a drink or something to eat.

The blonde took her usual break during the hottest part of the day and Julie took a dip in the ocean with Roger. To her relief he made no further mention of getting back together, and for this she was grateful; it certainly saved her having to deal with another set of emotions.

'Do you think we're going to have a storm?' she asked later in the afternoon. It seemed oppressively warm, more so than usual. They had gone out to the lagoon and he had helped her in, and was constantly attentive at her side.

'I wouldn't think so,' he said, shading his eyes and looking at the cloudless blue sky. 'It's the wrong time of year. January to April is the rainy season, I believe. It's also the hottest. It hardly ever rains otherwise.'

'Are you saying it's cooler now than it was a few weeks ago?' she asked, eyes wide.

'Apparently.'

'Then thank goodness I won't be here when it gets hot again,' she said with fervour. 'I don't think I could stand it.'

'Do you think Cameron *will* change his mind and let you stay on?' he asked. 'It seems to me a great pity to get rid of two very good people simply because of a little harmless deception.'

'It wasn't little to Cameron,' she admitted ruefully. 'If it wasn't for his book we'd have both been home by now.'

He put his hand on hers. 'I'm sorry he's giving you a hard time, Julie. I wish you'd let me say something to him.'

'No.' She shook her head firmly. 'We brought it on ourselves, we have to suffer the consequences.'

'But——'

'I don't want to discuss it any more, Roger.'

That evening Roger again joined Alex and Cameron in their customary swim, and Ian too. Surprisingly the girl appeared to enjoy the company of all the men— while Julie was left to work in the kitchen.

She noticed, in the days that followed, that Cameron seemed to be making a point of watching her and Roger very closely. Perhaps it was because he couldn't understand why his friend should give her another chance? His opinion of her was absolutely rock-bottom, and the more she thought about it the more depressed Julie became.

Deliberately, though, she kept her feelings hidden, playing up to Roger for all she was worth. And then came the day she announced that she was well enough to recommence typing his book.

They had finished their evening meal, Roger and Ian

had drifted away to talk to Rick and Lee, who had come wandering along the beach, and she was for once left alone with Cameron.

Instead of looking pleased, as she had expected, Cameron's brows rose in a derogatory manner. 'I thought this moment would never come.'

Julie frowned. 'What do you mean?'

'I thought that with Roger here you would play for more time. Just think, Julie, no more days spent sunning yourself in his company, no more days swimming together and whispering sweet words of love.'

'I've not been feigning it,' she protested vehemently. 'Do you really think I like sitting watching Alex doing my work? I enjoyed it, Cameron, I want to get back to it.'

Brows lifted sceptically. 'You sound serious.'

'I am serious,' she insisted. 'I'll start tomorrow, so you'd better tell Alex. Rick and Lee have been getting rather restless; I imagine they'll be glad to move on.'

'And is Roger going too?' he asked drily. 'Will we at last get back to normal?'

Nothing would ever be normal again, thought Julie. 'I imagine so,' she said wearily.

'You mean you haven't told him yet of your decision to start work again?'

'No.'

'But you will tonight? There'll be a charming little goodbye scene. Maybe he'll even spend the night in your tent. Is that what you plan, Julie?' He sounded bitter and angry, and Julie could not understand why.

Roger's voice suddenly interrupted them. Neither had noticed that he was back. 'I know I shouldn't be listening,' he said, 'but I think you've got hold of the wrong end of the stick, my friend. Julie and I finished a long time ago.'

Cameron turned cold eyes in Roger's direction. 'But you made it up again?'

Roger frowned and looked questioningly at Julie. She shook her head, trying to tell him not to say anything, but in vain. 'Yes, we made it up,' he said. 'But we're simply friends now, that is all. Whatever else we had going between us has gone, surely you knew that? I did ask Julie if we could get back together but she didn't want to, and I don't blame her. I did her a terrible injustice and I shall never forgive myself.'

Cameron frowned harshly. 'An injustice?' he queried. 'What are you talking about?'

It was Roger's turn to frown. 'Julie hasn't told you?'

'Told me what, for heaven's sake?' Cameron barked.

Roger took a seat beside them. 'She didn't two-time me, as I thought. She wasn't having an affair with someone else behind my back. I got the whole story wrong.'

Cameron's eyes narrowed as he looked from Roger to Julie. 'Is this the truth?'

She nodded, but wished Roger had kept his mouth shut. What good would all this do?

'Julie is a most loyal and wonderful person,' went on Roger staunchly. 'Look what she did for Ian. And you, my friend, had better apologise to her for your abominable behaviour. I've wanted to say something to you for days but Julie wouldn't let me. You're hurting her, man. I'm amazed she still wants to stay and type your book.'

Julie put her hand on Roger's and shook her head. 'Please, you're embarrassing me.'

He shrugged. 'OK, I've said enough; I'll leave you

two to talk. I think I might go and have a chat with Alex. I've taken rather a fancy to that young lady. Would I be stepping on your toes, Cameron, if I gave her my address so that I can see her when she travels on to England?'

Julie had had no idea that Roger was interested in Alex. This was a surprise. Was it the real reason he had come back? Not because of herself? It was an intriguing thought, and if that was the case he must have been deeply disappointed when he saw Alex making a play for Cameron.

And to her even more profound bewilderment Cameron smiled, a warm, pleased smile. 'Not at all, Roger. Feel free.'

'I thought you fancied Alex?' she questioned once Roger had sauntered away, and before she could stop herself.

Brows lifted. 'Did I give that impression?'

'Most definitely.'

'Did it bother you, Julie?'

Was this the time for honesty? She decided it wasn't; it could only lead to her own humiliation. She lifted her shoulders. 'Not in the least. What you do is your own affair.'

A muscle pulsed in his jaw, and a shadow of anger darkened his eyes. 'You really don't have a very high opinion of me, do you?'

'The same as you never had one of me,' she returned forcibly.

He growled. 'Why the devil did you let me believe that you and Roger had got back together?'

'Self-preservation, I guess,' she answered with a shrug.

A puzzled frown drew his black brows together. 'I don't understand.'

How could she tell him that it was because she loved him? How could she confess such a thing to a man who had no feelings for her except lust?

'Julie, answer me,' he said urgently, softly. 'Why still further deception?'

She winced at his choice of word. 'Because—because I thought it would—keep you away from me,' she whispered painfully.

'Is that you want?' He had stilled, everything about him was motionless—except for the muscle jerking in his jaw.

What could she say? She wanted to be honest, she wanted to tell him the truth, she wanted to bare her heart—but at what cost and for what good? She swallowed with difficulty. 'Not really.'

'But—you would prefer I didn't touch you or kiss you ever again?'

She closed her eyes, squirming uncomfortably in her seat. 'Not that either.'

'Then *what*, Julie?' His voice, much louder now, made her eyes snap open.

'I just don't like being abused. I wish that——'

'Abused?' he interjected harshly. 'Is that how you saw my kisses, as abuse?'

Almost imperceptibly, Julie nodded.

His fist crashed down on the table so violently and unexpectedly that she jumped, and her heart leapt in fear. It was a much more uncontrolled action than the last time he had done it.

'Let us get matters straight, right here and now,' he thundered. 'I never forced myself on you. You were always a willing participant. More than willing, in fact.

I actually—foolishly, it would appear—got the impression that you enjoyed kissing me.'

I did. I do, she answered silently. 'You once said that it was lust,' she whispered, pain so sharp in her heart that it was almost physical.

'I said that?' he queried fiercely. 'I don't remember. If I did it was a figure of speech; it meant nothing, certainly not that my interest in you was purely sexual. Lord, Julie, surely you know me better than that?'

'I don't think I know you at all,' she answered miserably.

'Then perhaps I should tell you how I feel.'

Her heart drummed a tattoo. Julie was not sure she was ready for this. It could sound the death-knell for any hopes.

'Julie.' He took her hand across the table, holding it in both of his. 'Look at me, Julie.'

With difficulty, she obeyed.

'Do you know why I was so angry when I finally forced you to admit that you weren't married to Ian?'

'Because you—hated the deceit?' she suggested.

'No—yes, but it wasn't that.' He shook his head firmly. 'It was because of my pent-up feelings, because, my dear girl, I'd fallen madly in love with you and was compelled to keep it bottled up. I was so damned frustrated it was destroying me, totally and utterly. I willed you to tell me the truth. I tried everything within my power to make you admit it, apart from asking you outright. God, Julie, I wanted to strangle you.'

He loved her! He *loved* her! Julie felt her heart singing; the words kept playing in her mind. It was sweet, sweet music. Cameron loved her. He loved her—he loved her.

'Answer me, dammit. Say something, Julie, even if it's only to laugh in my face.'

She looked at him then, wonderingly, seeing the hurt and the uncertainty, the fear still pounding in his brain. 'If you love me,' she said huskily, 'why didn't you say anything when the whole unfortunate story came out?'

'Because, God help me, I wanted to punish you,' he growled. 'I wanted to hurt you as I had been hurt. Besides, you said you were back with Roger, and when he turned up again it seemed to prove it. I'd lost you before I'd even had you. Damn, Julie. You've no idea how much I've suffered.'

And he was still suffering. There were still lines of pain furrowing his brow, behind his eyes, tightening his mouth; the whole of him was as tense as a bow-string.

'I never expected to meet someone like you,' he said, more quietly now, 'someone who loves the islands like I do, someone who has fitted in so well that when you depart it will leave a great void in my life.'

'I don't have to go,' she whispered. 'Ever.'

His head jerked, and his eyes pierced hers. 'What are you saying? That you'd be prepared to stay and do my typing on a permanent basis? Hell, Julie, I couldn't stand that, not feeling as I——'

'More than just your typing,' she interrupted softly.

He frowned. 'Make yourself clear.'

She swallowed painfully, and licked suddenly dry lips. 'I'm saying, Cameron, that—I love you too.'

He let go her hand and sat back in his chair, as though he needed the space to think clearly. 'Did you just say what I thought you said?' It was his turn to speak quietly and hoarsely.

'Yes.' Every pulse raced, every part of her was sensitised, and all she wanted was to hear him say again that he loved her. It was her prayer answered, a dream beyond all expectations.

'Is it the truth, Julie?'

She closed her eyes and nodded, and when she looked at him again there was an agony of longing in his eyes.

'How can it be, when I've been such a bastard to you?'

She gave a twisted smile. 'How can it be when you've always sworn never to fall in love? When I swore there would never be anyone else after Roger? These things seem to happen whether we want them to or not.'

'Do you really love me?'

'Yes, Cameron,' she answered simply, 'with all my heart.'

He got up then, and Julie rose too, and locked in each other's arms they kissed, their first kiss given in true love. Julie felt herself soaring into space, felt her whole body being uplifted. She felt exhilarated, and crushed also by the intenseness of her love for this man. Could it really be true?

When he lifted his head, she looked at him and said, 'Tell me I'm not dreaming.'

'If you are, then so am I,' he said gruffly. 'God, you feel good.' Another hungry kiss took up several more minutes.

'Was there really nothing between you and Alex?' she asked when he gave her breathing space. 'I saw her coming from your tent one night and——'

He groaned. 'Dammit, I admit I flirted with her—I wanted to make you jealous—but she's only a kid. She was experimenting, I think. I let her down gently. Nothing happened, I assure you, and she certainly wasn't serious about me.'

'You did make me jealous,' she admitted. 'I felt quite ill with it at times.'

'Lord, I was blind,' he growled. 'Roger had painted such a black picture of you, before I even met you, so when you turned up I refused to see anything other than the fact that you responded to me in a sexual manner. I didn't think it went any deeper—I thought you had no morals; I even thought you were after Jake.' He grimaced painfully. 'I *am* guilty of abusing you, Julie, and I'm deeply ashamed. I wouldn't blame you if you never forgave me.'

'I already have,' she whispered, her love for this handsome man shining in her eyes.

'You never forgave Roger.'

She frowned. 'What makes you say that?'

'Because you wouldn't take him back, even after he'd admitted that he was wrong.'

A rueful smile twisted her lips. 'I guess that means I never truly loved him.'

He seemed satisfied with her answer. 'How much do you love me, Julie?'

'Enough for all time,' she answered, content now in the knowledge that Cameron loved her also.

Another kiss, another journey into space, and then he said, 'I don't even care now if my book doesn't get finished. It's you I care about, dearest Julie. You I love, you I want to marry. Could you really live out here?'

'Wherever you are I want to be,' she answered sincerely.

'You won't hanker after England, and a house and babies?'

'Not until you're ready,' she told him.

He pulled a surprised face—surprise at himself, not

her. 'I guess I might be ready sooner than I ever thought. Was it fate that sent you to me, my sweet Julie?'

She grinned. 'I guess it was my ambitious brother. I'm sorry for the pretence, I really am. I hated it. It went against every principle I hold, and I was always so scared of you finding out.'

'You had no idea that I already knew?'

'Oh, yes,' she admitted, 'I was pretty sure; you dropped enough hints, but I couldn't let Ian down. I had to carry on with it for his sake.'

He looked at her long and hard. 'I have to admit it was a very admirable thing to do. Not many sisters would.'

'I love him,' she answered simply.

'And I love you,' he muttered darkly. 'It's been hell, waiting for you to confess, and I think you should know that was the reason I put you in separate tents.'

'I'm glad you did,' she said huskily.

'It's been the most frustrating time of my life,' he growled. 'I was attracted to you the first moment, the first second I set eyes on you, and you were so delightfully, righteously angry at times. "I have every intention of tying my hair back just as soon as I've had a shower," you said, so uptightly. God, you were beautiful.'

'I felt something for you too,' she admitted. 'I suppose our only consolation is that if I hadn't masqueraded as Ian's wife I would never have come out here and we would never have met.' It was something she had thought of often.

'I guess, in a way, he did us both a favour,' Cameron agreed. 'And of course he'll stay on now, for as long as he likes. He's proving to be a very valuable member of our research team. What do you think he'll say to our news?'

'He already knows I love you,' she confessed.

Cameron looked surprised. 'He does?'

'Yes.'

'And Roger? Does he know too? Was that why he just attacked me? Am I the last to know?' But he didn't look angry.

Julie shook her head. 'No, Roger doesn't know. He still thinks you're a sworn bachelor.'

'All it took was a black-haired beauty in high heels — a hazel-eyed witch. You cast your spell on me, Julie. I want us to get married without delay.'

'I'll get married right here on this island, if that's what you want,' she said, gazing adoringly into his eyes. 'Or we could go back to England and have a big white wedding with our——'

'No!' he stated emphatically. 'Here, tomorrow — or at least as soon as it can be arranged. I'm not waiting. I'm not prepared to take the risk that someone else might snatch you from beneath my nose.'

'That won't happen, my handsome Cameron,' she said with a confident smile. 'You're my once in a lifetime man. It's you or no one, but I'll only marry you if you assure me it will last forever.'

He looked sad for a moment. 'I guess that's what our parents thought, what most people think when they get married. But if it's within my power to make you happy for the rest of your life, then that's what I shall do. I've waited too long to make a mistake. I love you, Julie, and I always will, and that is a promise.'

It was her promise to Cameron too, and as they walked hand in hand on the white coral shore of what had to be the most beautiful island in the world, her heart was singing.

# GET 4 BOOKS
# AND A MYSTERY GIFT

Return this coupon and we'll send you 4 Mills & Boon Romances and a mystery gift absolutely FREE! We'll even pay the postage and packing for you.

We're making you this offer to introduce you to the benefits of Reader Service: FREE home delivery of brand-new Mills & Boon romances, at least a month before they are available in the shops, FREE gifts and a monthly Newsletter packed with information.

Accepting these FREE books and gift places you under no obligation to buy, you may cancel at any time, even after receiving just your free shipment. Simply complete the coupon below and send it to:

MILLS & BOON READER SERVICE, FREEPOST, CROYDON, SURREY, CR9 3WZ.

## No stamp needed

Yes, please send me 4 free Mills & Boon Romances and a mystery gift. I understand that unless you hear from me, I will receive 6 superb new titles every month for just £1.99* each postage and packing free. I am under no obligation to purchase any books and I may cancel or suspend my subscription at any time, but the free books and gifts will be mine to keep in any case. (I am over 18 years of age)

1EP6R

Ms/Mrs/Miss/Mr _____

Address _____

_____

_____ Postcode _____

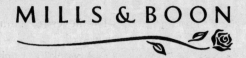

# MILLS & BOON

## Next Month's Romances

Each month you can choose from a wide variety of romance with Mills & Boon. Below are the new titles to look out for next month.

| | |
|---|---|
| ANGRY DESIRE | Charlotte Lamb |
| THE VALENTINE CHILD | Jacqueline Baird |
| THE UNFAITHFUL WIFE | Lynne Graham |
| A KISS TO REMEMBER | Miranda Lee |
| GUARDIAN GROOM | Sandra Marton |
| PRIVATE DANCER | Eva Rutland |
| THE MARRIAGE SOLUTION | Helen Brooks |
| SECOND HONEYMOON | Sandra Field |
| MARRIAGE VOWS | Rosalie Ash |
| THE WEDDING DECEPTION | Kay Thorpe |
| THE HERO TRAP | Rosemary Badger |
| FORSAKING ALL OTHERS | Susanne McCarthy |
| RELENTLESS SEDUCTION | Kim Lawrence |
| PILLOW TALK | Rebecca King |
| EVERY WOMAN'S DREAM | Bethany Campbell |
| A BRIDE FOR RANSOM | Renee Roszel |